xxxHOLiC :ANOTHERHOLiC
LANDOLT-RING AEROSOL

WRITTEN BY

ORIGINAL CONCEPT AND
ILLUSTRATIONS BY
CLAMP

TRANSLATED BY ANDREW CUNNINGHAM

BALLANTINE BOOKS | NEW YORK

A Del Rey Manga / Kodansha Hardcover Original

xxxHOLiC: ANOTHERHOLiC: Landolt-Ring Aerosol copyright © 2006
by CLAMP / NISIOISIN
English translation copyright © 2008 by CLAMP / NISIOISIN

Published in the United States by Del Rey Books, an imprint of
The Random House Publishing Group, a division of Random House, Inc., New York.

DEL REY is a registered trademark and the Del Rey colophon
is a trademark of Random House, Inc.

Publication rights arranged through Kodansha Ltd.

First published in Japan in 2006 by Kodansha Ltd., Tokyo

ISBN 978-0-345-50518-7

Printed in the United States of America on acid-free paper

www.delreymanga.com

9 8 7 6 5 4 3 2 1

Translator: Andrew Cunningham

First Edition

CONTENTS

LIST OF CHARACTERS

Yûko Ichihara: Shop owner

Kimihiro Watanuki: High school student

Shizuka Dômeki: High school student

Himawari Kunogi: High school student

Sekô Serizawa: High school student

Nurie Kushimura: Employee

Hôseki Hikage: College student

Kokyû Shikasaka: College student

Basara Bakemachi: Physicist

"No, ghosts are real. You can see them, touch them, and hear them. But they do not exist. Which is why science ignores them. But to claim they are a fabrication and do not exist because science ignores them is a mistake. Because ghosts are real."

—NATSUHIKO KYÔGOKU, *UBUME NO NATSU*

* *Natsuhiko Kyôgoku* Extremely successful author of supernatural mysteries. *Ubume no Natsu*/Summer of the Ubume (Kodansha Ltd., 2003) was his first novel. He is known for very long books containing elaborate philosophical and psychological reinterpretations of Japanese folklore, and for a very methodical and exacting approach to writing. He hates it when a sentence runs onto the next page, and lays out all his works himself to make sure that never happens, revising the works extensively for each new edition.

An *Ubume*, according to folklore, is a bird with a woman's head that steals newborn babies. This particular quote posed a bit of a translation problem; the first and last sentences use the word "*iru*," which means "to be," while the third and fifth sentence use the noun "exist." To keep the distinction, I was unable to translate "*iru*" as "exist." It took quite a while to figure out another way of saying the same thing that kept the connotation and remained true to the context of this quote in the original novel.

—heartless eyes.

My first impression of the black-haired woman, Yûko Ichihara, settled on that phrase.

—frightening eyes.

—cruel eyes.

—bewitching eyes.

—hard eyes.

—eyes that looked at you as though you were less than human.

—eyes that looked at you from the other side.

—eyes that looked right through you.

—eyes that appraised you.

—eyes that measured the world in reverse.

—eyes that denied the way of the world.

That sort of eyes.

Unable to stand having those eyes focused on me, and unable to continue staring back at them, I consciously dropped my gaze.

It settled on the cup of coffee in front of me.

That boy, Kimihiro Watanuki, had made it for me; he had asked if I wanted coffee or tea the moment I sat down, and I had said coffee.

Even though I wanted tea.

I refused milk and sugar.

Even though bitter coffee is undrinkable.

The same coffee sat in front of her. She had said nothing except to give me her name, just sat there staring at me. But I was sure that Ichihara-san had wanted to drink coffee, and did not require either milk or sugar.

Steam rose from the black liquid.

Pitch-black liquid.

Ooh . . .

If I flung this liquid at her, how would her expression change? What kind of eyes would look at me then?

I knew I should not do that.

She would be angry—and I had only just met her.

I was here only because Watanuki-kun had been nice enough to bring me. I wasn't sure if she could provide counseling or what, but there was absolutely no connection between me and Ichihara-san . . .

"Call me Yûko," she said.

Just as my fingers had touched the cup's handle, absently seeking a way to fill the silence, Ichihara-san corrected me, even though I had never said her name aloud.

"And—that thing you were about to do? Don't," she snapped.

I looked up, surprised.

Her eyes were the same.

Still staring fixedly at me.

Then Yûko Ichihara smiled faintly. "Or perhaps . . . *this* way of putting things would work better with you, Nurie Kushimura-san.

———

"Go ahead. I dare you."

■ ■ ■ ■

There are a great many strange things in the world.

———

But no matter how odd . . .

How incredible something may be . . .

———

If a human does not touch it . . .
If a human does not see it . . .
If a human is not involved with it . . .

———

It is simply a phenomenon.
Simply a matter that will fade with time.

———

Humans.
Mankind.
Homo sapiens.

———

Humans are the most profoundly mysterious living things in the world!

■　■　■　■

Kimihiro Watanuki was perceptive.

Not in the sense that he possessed any superhuman penetrative insight. He did not have a knack for reading personality and character, and never said anything along the lines of "He might act thuggish, but he'll grow into a strong leader eventually. But that may well mean he becomes a powerful enemy." Or "You can trust her. The rough way she talks is just a pose, and deep down she's really very docile. It would help if she could learn to forgive herself."

He was not insightful, merely perceptive.

He did not see people, but spirits.

Spirits: Things which are always around but cannot normally be seen.

Things not of this world.

Things that, perhaps, were not meant to be seen.

But Kimihiro Watanuki could see them clearly.

This was a problem for him.

It was not an ability, simply a faculty, innate and not acquired, resulting not from conscious thought but from the flow of blood through his body. It was a vision that was always with him—a problem that nothing he did would ever solve. Seeing alone was bad enough, but there were also spirits that came to him, drawn by his blood, which always caused an unholy mess.

A mess he had to clean up.

He had done everything he could, but there had never been anything he could do in the first place. It would have made sense just to give up, and that might well have been the best thing he could do. But even so, even in full knowledge of that, there was not a day when he didn't wish.

If only I couldn't see.

That wish went through his head every day.

But it was less a wish than a prayer.

———

A few months ago, someone had promised to grant his wish.

———

"This has got to be a joke," Kimihiro Watanuki muttered. No, the way he spit out the words was closer to a snarl, and his shoulders were shaking with rage. He was standing in front of the coin lockers outside the gates of JR Glass Station, about a ten-minute train ride east of the station closest to his high school, Cross Private School. The people around him had collectively decided to go out of their way to avoid his vicinity.

He was holding a letter in his hand.

A very short letter.

FAKE GLASSES (NOT AN EYEPATCH).

Perhaps more of a memo than a letter.

Watanuki glanced up again at the locker in front of him: No. 45.

The memo had been inside the locker.

"She could have just *said* this! Why does she always have to be so roundabout—and what the hell does 'Fake glasses (not an eyepatch)' mean? Nobody in the universe would mix those two things up! Oh, wait, she's talking about Date Masamune, who founded that place where they make the *Zunda Mochi* . . . Sendai. Aggh! That's such a reach I can't even think of a comeback!"

It was evening, rush hour.

Kimihiro Watanuki's very audible fury directed at someone who was not even there sent people moving swiftly away from him like an ebb tide, but he was in no mood to notice or care.

The day before, his employer had given him a key. The number 45 was inscribed on the key—the key to this locker.

° *JR Glass Station*   Not a real station. NISIOISIN actually uses the kanji for "glass" (or *Gurasu*—glass being a word imported back when they were still creating kanji readings for foreign words). In Japan, the xxxHOLiC novel and NISIOISIN's *Death Note* novel were published at the same time, and there is also a mention of a Glass Station in LA in the *Death Note* novel.

° *Date Masamune*   Samurai, founder of the city of Sendai. Sendai—capital of Miyage Prefecture—is famous for a snack called *Zunda Mochi*, which appears to consist of beaten rice (*mochi*) and green soy beans. Date was a skilled tactician who had only one eye; he was called the one-eyed dragon because of this. The rather tenuous connection to fake glasses comes from the word *Date*, which means "dandy," but when combined with the word for glasses (*megane*) becomes "fake glasses." Date Megane and Date Masamune are not very easy to confuse, but the Date part does have the same kanji.

His employer—although besides Watanuki she oversaw only a paiyukimir of girls who may or may not have qualified as employees and a sort of pet thing like a black Yukimi Dai-fuku—had given him no details or instructions beyond, "Go open that door for me."

"All that work I put into figuring out that this key came from the lockers outside Glass Station, and all I find is an-other order!? Is this a game for elementary school kids?"

No amount of screaming in rage could heal the frustra-tion.

All of his effort boiled down to his employer ordering him to find a pair of fake glasses. He did not venture to dream that things would end with the acquisition of said phony specta-cles; that quest would soon be followed by some new order, which would in turn be followed by another, and another . . .

"She's just toying with me. . . . This has absolutely noth-ing to do with my actual job."

His shoulders stopped shaking, and he slumped.

He appeared to have come to terms with it.

Indeed, no matter how absurd, no matter how obviously the request served her own amusement, as long as the orders came from his employer—Yûko Ichihara—Watanuki had no choice but to obey.

Absolute obedience.

Why? Because it was a fair price.

The price he had to pay before his eyes would stop seeing.

"Hahhh . . ."

Yûko Ichihara's shop, where Kimihiro Watanuki worked,

° *Yukimi Daifuku* Ice cream wrapped in *mochi.*

was a shop that could make wishes come true. As long as one paid a reasonable price, no matter how extravagant or fantastic the wish—even if you wished to not see spirits, to not have blood that attracted spirits—this shop could fulfill your request.

A shop that granted wishes.

"Except the way she's working me, it might just be faster to go out collecting dragonballs. Does she actually mean to grant my wish?"

Watanuki had worked for Yûko for several months now and was quite sure that she had the ability to grant wishes in return for that fair price. He was well aware of the extent of her power.

But he had his doubts about her intentions.

"As much as she goes on about fair prices, she can't possibly expect me to work for free . . . but what does she want with fake glasses? She gonna wear them? Yûko-san in fake glasses? Or is there some massive Warashibe Chôja–style success lurking in my future? Will I end up rich? Gosh, what an exciting prospect. Damn it. Anyway . . ."

He could not stand here fuming forever.

With that in mind, Watanuki forced himself to think. He had never bought a pair of fake glasses before, or even entertained a fleeting desire to do so, and literally had no idea where he could purchase such a thing. "Fake" meant that the lenses were just glass, so they could hardly be as expensive as functional spectacles. If she wanted sunglasses, he was sure the message would have said as much, so he should avoid tinted lenses. Which meant, in short—

* *Warashibe Chôja* Japanese folktale in which a poor boy trades one object for another until he ends up rich.

"I don't know this area well, but surely there's one around. They would have it."

—the obvious first stop.

A hundred-yen shop.

There was one in every area with a certain level of population, and they generally carried quite a wide selection of products, all of which cost only a hundred yen. Since he had no idea where Yûko's demands would take him next, it seemed prudent to keep expenses to an absolute minimum, which a hundred yen certainly was.

He left Glass Station, looking for a hundred-yen shop.

Luckily, he found one just across the street. He went down the sidewalk, into the store, and headed for the everyday goods section. There were any number of frames so bizarre Watanuki was sure no one in the country would ever dream of wearing them, but among them he found what he was looking for.

"They've got glasses for old people too. . . . Quite a time we live in. Well . . . should probably get one that doesn't look too cheap . . . Hmm, guess there are limits to what you can get for a hundred yen. Red feels right, somehow . . ."

He bought them. With tax, the price came to 105 yen. He was out of change, and had to pay with a thousand-yen bill, which left him carrying around a fistful of coins. Watanuki always felt a little empty, like he brought it on himself, whenever he got a lot of change.

He left the shop and waited. For his next orders.

He had the fake glasses, completing the mission provided by the locker. Watanuki waited to see just how his next orders would arrive, uncharacteristically excited.

From behind? From the sky? From underground? Or directly into his head, supersonically . . . ?

Nothing.

Apparently the fake glasses completed Yûko's requests for the day.

"Is that it? I'm never gonna be rich? Such a shame," he said softly, well aware of how selfish a line of thought that was. Watanuki sighed deeply. It was already late, and he had to deliver the fake glasses to Yûko and then make her dinner before he could get off work. How much had he earned toward his wish that day? He felt like an RPG character wandering aimlessly around the dungeon, trying to raise his level from 98 to 99. A living example of the the phrase "getting nowhere."

"Wonder if she'd make me a stamp card . . . then at least I'd have some idea how much progress I'm making."

Or was his goal so far off that seeing it was more depressing than not seeing it? It was said that even the longest journey begins with a single step, but if you counted each of those steps nearly everyone would give up long before they completed the journey.

What he needed to think about right now, assuming this had all been an elaborate joke on Yûko-san's part, was how, exactly, upon his return to the shop, he should react to the joke crashing in a massive apocalypse of flame. He needed to decide just what kind of reaction he should display once he was back at the shop. The joke was a bad one and the timing of it so off that this was a task rather more difficult than tracking down "Date Masamune's eyepatch."

He headed for the crosswalk.

The light was red.

Cars were zipping by, so, naturally, Watanuki stopped. Four or five other people were waiting for the light to change as well.

"Mm?"

One of them caught his attention.

He looked closer.

She was biting her lower lip . . .

. . . looking very, very desperate.

But that was not what drew Watanuki's eye. Not that at all.

She was a rather petite woman, and on her thin shoulder . . .

———

. . . *something.*

———

By the time he noticed, it was too late.

Too late to do anything.

The woman flung herself out into traffic.

■ ■ ■ ■

Oh.

I did it again.

When I woke up in the hospital bed I plunged instantly into a tortuous well of self-loathing. Tomorrow was a very important day— No, I'd been out too long. Today.

Today was a very important day.

What was I doing in a hospital bed?

I looked out the window.

I couldn't see from here.

But right now, at work, Hyôdô-kun must be doing the new project presentation, the one I was supposed to do, the one I should have been doing. That was what we had planned in case of an emergency, an emergency that should never have come to pass.

I'd caused problems for them all again.

We had all worked so hard to get that plan ready. . . . I knew Hyôdô-kun would do a good job covering for me, but that wasn't the point.

I had done it again.

Let myself do it—do what I knew I should not do.

Just as I had ever since I was a child.

———

I longed to violate taboos.

———

According to the nurse, I had been waiting at a crosswalk, then suddenly jumped out into traffic. I had no memories of the accident—but even without those memories, I knew myself.

I had jumped out into traffic at a red light. I had done the same thing, or other things very similar, over and over, my whole life.

Fortunately, this time I had got off with a fracture of my left arm. Probably because I'd been hit by a scooter.

But if it had not been a scooter, I would have died.

Maybe that would have been better. Frankly, the fact that I had survived this long was miraculous. The world's most pointless miracle.

When I was in elementary school, I jumped out the classroom window. Like the main character in that famous novel. For that matter, I had touched blades to my fingers more than a few times. As an adolescent I'd tried my hand at cutting my wrist, though only once.

° *Famous novel*   Soseki Natsume's classic *Botchan*. The main character jumped out of the classroom window at the beginning of the story.

But that once might have been enough.

I might have died.

People asked me, "Why did you do that?"

They scolded me. "You shouldn't do things like that!"

But were they right?

Everyone had feelings like mine occasionally. Like the urge to pull the fire alarm in the school hallway (I had done so countless times before graduating high school) or the urge to leap in front of the train as it pulled into the station, wind gusting, buzzer sounding (I always had to fight myself). If you climb up somewhere high, do you never wonder what it would be like to jump off? (I'm battling those feelings before I even start to climb.)

Everyone felt like that sometimes, some more than others.

No exceptions.

I just felt like that more than most.

My urges were abundant and vast.

I knew that, I was very, very aware of that, but even knowing that, even aware of that, there was nothing I could do about it, which was exactly why I called such feelings urges.

Urges.

Urges, destructive urges.

To put it simply, it was the commonplace idea of the button that says DON'T PUSH taken to extremes. How many people could honestly say they would not push that button?

As for me . . .

I promise I would push it.

Junior High Entrance Exams.

The day of the test for a famous private school I'd been assured I would be able to pass—I feigned illness, and spent the day lying in bed at home. High school entrance exams were the same. I ended up at ordinary public schools for both junior and senior high. If someone had asked me why I needed to pretend I was sick, the only thing I could have said was that I wanted to see what would happen if you got sick on such an important day.

When it came time to go to college, I deliberately didn't write my name on the application for my first choice school . . . no, maybe I did write it, but either way, I ended up at my safety school.

For the same reason.

Yes. Yes, I know.

The fact that I have managed to survive to the age of twenty-seven cannot be described by any word except *miraculous*. Presumably my reason barely managed to restrain my emotions—but that reason is starting to get a little threadbare. The conflict between the two is swiftly reaching its limit.

While I'd caused a lot of problems for myself, I *had* managed to avoid any massive failures at work so far. And while it will sound like I'm bragging, if this presentation had been a success, it would undoubtedly have opened the door to a promotion.

Instead, I had given that chance to my subordinate. That interpretation of my behavior makes it a lot easier for me to take. It always felt comfortable to coddle myself. It was my left arm I'd fractured, so my injury wouldn't be that big a problem at work; it was Friday, and I'd probably be back at work next week.

But that thought brought them back again.

Brought back the urges.

What if?

What if next week I did not go back to work, if I never went to work again?

Oh, that would be awful.

That plan involved things that only I could do. Even if Hyôdô-kun nailed the presentation, the plan itself would probably be squashed. And the other members of my group would pay the price; no one would be talking about promotion anymore.

Did I care?

It's not as though this company had been my first choice.

It was my second.

At the interview for my first choice I had tripped and fallen down — I can still remember the disgusted looks the interviewers gave me. But they had never suspected that I had fallen over deliberately.

So . . .

. . . could I just stop going to work?

Oh, no.

No, stop thinking about it.

I didn't want to do that.

I didn't.

I didn't. I didn't. I didn't. I didn't. I didn't. I didn't. I didn't. I didn't. I didn't. I didn't. I didn't. I didn't. I didn't. I didn't. I didn't. I didn't. I didn't. I didn't.

I didn't — so I couldn't let myself.

I hadn't let myself screw up at work — that much was true.

But then I remembered . . .

When was that? Just after I started?

I put an important document through the shredder.

Deliberately, of course.

Disguised as a coincidence, so no one would know.

Because of that, everyone in the department had barely slept for a week—but we had managed to pull through.

It had been an important document, but not a critical one.

So it didn't count.

Neither did this event.

I would recover. I could make it up to everyone.

I could.

But then the second wave hit me.

What if?

When it was time for me to apologize, I insisted I'd done nothing wrong, and berated them all . . . what would they do then?

They were so nice.

How would they look at me?

———

Oh, I wanted to do that.

Urges like that possessed me.

They always had, since before I could remember.

———

But no more.

Let me be clear: I was neither self-destructive nor suicidal. That much I was sure of. I could deny that with confidence. I had as much reason to crave death or danger as anyone else—a love for roller coasters, nothing more than ordinary curiosity.

I just had these urges.

I just had these urges.

To violate taboos.

To do things I really shouldn't do.

There were all kinds of things that should matter more to me than those feelings—relationships, work, so many other things I should care about more—but here I was wondering what would happen if I jumped out the window of my hospital room.

They'd be mad at me.

I might even die.

But.

But that's why I wanted to.

———

I wanted to push the button marked DON'T PUSH.

———

"Why did you do that?"

"You shouldn't do things like that!"

That's why I wanted to.

Why? Because I wanted to.

That's all.

It had been a scooter, so I was still alive, and it was no big deal, but if it had been a dump truck there was no way I could have survived.

It was a miracle that I was alive.

So I thought . . .

Maybe things would be better if I were dead.

But if I died, how would that affect everyone else?

I managed to trample down the urge to jump out the window, and took a deep breath, preparing myself to fight the next urge.

There was a knock on the door, and a voice called out, "Kushimura-san! Can I come in?"

Must be the nurse.

I said sure.

A moment later, the door opened and the nurse came in, in her pink uniform . . . but she was not alone.

There was someone with her.

A boy in a school uniform, with glasses on.

I had seen him before.

But where?

———

He said his name was Kimihiro Watanuki.

■ ■ ■ ■

"Uh-huh. I see," the black-haired woman said ominously. "So that's why you skipped out on work without permission yesterday or even a phone call, and that's why you came to work late today without permission or even a phone call." Wreaths of smoke curled from her pipe, and her left hand toyed with the fake glasses Watanuki had purchased the day before for 105 yen (tax included).

Yûko Ichihara.

The owner of the shop that could grant any wish.

Owner, operator, whatever you wanted to call her, she was the one who employed Kimihiro Watanuki, and who would, in the future, be his salvation. If she wasn't, he was in trouble.

Some people called her the Dimension Witch, but he wasn't sure why. Her age and history were a mystery, and she would not even tell him her blood type, let alone her birthday. Even her name, Yûko Ichihara, was fake. Watanuki knew it was fake because she had told him as much when they first met, no more than five seconds after giving her name. The most brazen fake name around. Presumably her real name was something much more obviously sinister.

Yûko smirked. "Such a lot of bother."

"Nah. I'm glad you noticed. But did you need those glasses for something?"

"Not really," she said.

Innocently.

It really had been just a joke . . .

"Think of it as a scavenger hunt."

"So it was a scavenger hunt instead of a treasure hunt? Not a whole lot of difference. And I would greatly prefer if you could not waste my time on either. Just leads to trouble, frankly."

"But you can hardly say it was boring. For all your complaints, you enjoyed it. The moment you opened the locker, you must have thought, 'Seriously? Can this possibly be true?' "

"I did."

But probably not in the sense she meant it.

"You thought 'This is so cool♡!' "

"Except I am not a high school girl."

"Oh, how boring of you," she said, sounding disappointed.

She would have preferred him as a girl?

"Personally, I'd welcome an apology for being forced to participate in your pointless little game."

"Quite an attitude—you want an apology? There is nothing more pathetic than asking for an apology. Watanuki, I overestimated you."

"I'd prefer you revise your estimate of me based on something that actually matters."

"Nothing in this world is devoid of meaning, Watanuki. Even games," Yûko said decisively. She pointed her pipe at Watanuki. "How was she?"

"Who? You mean the girl I saw at the hospital?"

Yesterday.

While he stood at the crosswalk, on his way home after successfully purchasing the fake spectacles in the hundred-yen shop near JR Glass Station, a woman had suddenly thrown herself into traffic.

Watanuki had called the ambulance.

He had also gone with her to the hospital and contacted her family.

And today, after school, before coming to work at the shop that granted wishes, he had bought flowers and gone to see Nurie Kushimura in the hospital.

As a result of which . . .

He had earned black marks for skipping work and arriving late.

But Yûko Ichihara did not seem the type to be particularly put out by something like that. Indeed, she seemed more likely to use the fact that Watanuki had not even bothered thinking up a good excuse for his behavior as leverage.

But now?

She asked about the woman.

"Of course, the girl at the hospital. Watanuki, you said there was something on her shoulder."

"Yeah . . . but I might just have been seeing things. I mean, I was looking out of the corner of my eye—"

"But," Yûko interrupted, "you thought you 'saw' it."

He had.

"Uh, but . . . it was just a glimpse, that's all. It might have been something sewn on her shoulder bag that reflected the streetlights into my eyes . . ."

"But," Yûko said again, "you don't think it was."

He did not.

"That's why you went to see her today, that's why you talked to her."

That was true, but how she could be so sure was beyond him.

Watanuki was extremely undecided about whether he should relate the contents of that conversation to Yûko. If this were the kind of mystery novel found in every home—"A chance encounter involves Watson in a most troubling affair. Whereupon gallant Holmes arrives to cut through all complications and solve the matter with alacrity."—consulting Yûko would be faster, but this was precisely the kind of problem he did not want to bring to her attention.

Putting aside the comparison to Holmes, Yûko Ichihara was fundamentally not reliable.

And even if you chose to rely on her . . . you needed to pay a fair price.

And Yûko could be outright mean when it came to that.

The word *volunteer* was not in her dictionary.

Over the last few months Watanuki had not once borne witness to the sight of Yûko doing anything without payment. Nothing available in this shop was ever for free.

She always extracted payment, to the point of heartlessness.

That went for Watanuki . . .

. . . and it would go for the woman as well.

Watanuki was currently carrying out his own payment, and occasionally, very occasionally, he wondered: Even if his wish were granted, what she took in return was of equal value, and in the end . . . did it really make a difference whether the wish was granted or not?

His eyes.

The eyes that saw spirits.

When he had paid the price, and his eyes could no longer see . . . how much would he have lost in return?

The idea scared him.

So he always pushed it away.

Tried not to think about it.

But when it came to other people—that was different. Kimihiro Watanuki's feeling was that introducing people with wishes to Yûko Ichihara was something he never should do lightly.

If at all.

"Tell me about it, Watanuki. If this were *Doraemon*, I would be Doraemon, see?"

"If you're Doraemon, then mentioning the name of the show is redundant."

"And you, Watanuki, are Sewashi-kun."

"Not Nobita-kun!?"

"Are you Nobita-kun?"

"No . . . no, I'm not, but . . ."

"Then you must be Sewashi-kun."

° *Doraemon* A very famous children's manga and anime. The title character is a robot cat from the future, with items that can do almost anything hidden in his fourth-dimensional pocket. The main character, Nobita, is a rather helpless boy, prone to crying. Sewashi is Nobita's great-great-grandson, the man who sends Doraemon into the past. He appears only in the first few stories.

"I have to be one or the other?"

An extremely limited selection.

He couldn't even remember what kind of character Sewashi-kun *was*.

And hijacking the analogy — Yûko Ichihara was about as far from a character that had become a national icon as it was possible to be. Her position was much closer to that of the salesman wearing a funereal suit in another work by the same author. Anyway. He was Yûko's employee, and when he said to tell her about it, he had to talk. To his frequent regret, it was vividly clear which of them controlled the other, and beyond that, the situation he found himself in now was entirely the result of his own careless failure to call the shop yesterday before going to the hospital today. "You smell like flowers, Watanuki," Yûko said, driving him even further into the corner. "You should know better than to bring such heavily scented flowers to a hospital."

"Nah, that's not . . ."

"Oh? Not what?" Yûko purred, looking extremely confident. As if she hardly needed Watanuki to explain.

As if she already knew everything.

But if he pointed that out she would inevitably say something frustratingly Zen. Such as, "If you believe I know, then I probably do, but if not, I don't." She might not be deliberately attempting to cover the issue in smoke, but Watanuki would be coughing anyway.

° *Salesman in a suit* Fukuzo Moguro, the main character of *Warau Salesman* (*Smiling Salesman*) by Fujiko Fujio, who always wears a black suit. The story is famous for its cynicism and black humor, and has never been suitable for children. Watanuki associates Moguro's mean and dark character with Yûko's.

Not a pleasant sensation.

So he just answered her question.

"Um, so . . . this woman's name was Nurie Kushimura. In her late twenties, I think. *Kushi* is 'comb,' " he said, idly wondering whether Yûko actually needed him to explain the kanji but deciding that it was the normal thing to do. "*Mura* is 'village,' and her first name is 'paint' and 'picture.' "

"Hmm . . . is that her *real* name?"

"That's what was written on her hospital bed, so I assume so. Those charts are based on your proof of insurance."

"I see. Nurie Kushimura. What's her birthday?"

"I don't know."

"I see." Watanuki had been prepared for a scathing remark, but Yûko just nodded. "So, why is it that you smell of flowers? Were you randomly embraced by a woman wearing far too much perfume?"

"Of course not."

"I guessed as much. Then I shall assume that you have just begun wearing perfume."

"Please don't."

"Then why?"

"Um . . . well, when I gave her the flowers . . . Kushimura-san, um . . . hit me with them," Watanuki admitted, reluctantly.

"My!" Yûko exclaimed, as if she could not be happier. Her target acquired.

"Not many people have the privilege of being beaten with a bouquet when they come for a hospital visit. Only someone as hapless as you, Watanuki."

° *Nurie Kushimura*   NISIOISIN is famous for creating extremely odd names, and Nurie Kushimura is no exception.

"Hapless? Since when am I hapless?"

"You always were. I'm amazed you can even ask without blushing. If we removed the haplessness from you, what would remain? A Watanuki who is not hapless is like a Watanuki who was not born on April first."

"Like the vast majority of people named Watanuki?"

"I didn't mean them."

"Sigh . . . okay."

She hadn't meant them.

He knew that.

"In that case, Watanuki, why did she do that to you? Did you do something to make her mad? Make a silly joke, like 'Since this hospital was founded, not one patient has ever left alive'?"

"My life has not become so devoid of meaning that I would find such bizarre black humor amusing."

"Hmm. Then why?"

"Well . . . that is the weird part. Apparently . . . there was no reason."

"No reason."

Hit a visitor with flowers.

For no reason.

"Yes. After she hit me with the flowers, Kushimura-san apologized profusely. She said she didn't mean to do it, that she knew it was wrong."

A meaningful silence from Yûko.

She did not smile.

He'd known her for a while, but this look always unnerved him.

Trying to shake off that feeling, he cleared his throat. "So I talked to her a little more, and it sounds like she's been that way for a while. Habitually doing things she knows she shouldn't do. She insists it isn't self-destructive, but I found that hard to believe."

A button marked DON'T PUSH.

If she saw one . . . she would absolutely push it.

That was why she had jumped out into traffic the day before. It had meant that she would miss a major event at work, one that could lead to a promotion. That knowledge had led her to it.

Kimihiro Watanuki related everything Nurie Kushimura had told him. But she had been very flustered after smacking him with the flowers. Her version of the story had been rather scattered, and he was forced to summarize for coherency's sake. He was getting pretty good at that sort of thing.

Essentially . . .

. . . she violated taboos.

"It felt kind of like she is deliberately, intentionally wrecking her own life. Ever since she was a child. She calls it her 'urges'—which is at least the extent to which she is aware of herself. I couldn't begin to imagine how strong they really are. What do you make of it, Yûko-san? Are there any spirits that can do that to people?"

Just before she jumped into traffic.

The thing he'd seen on her shoulder.

What . . . was it?

"There are," Yûko said. "There are, or should I say, there is such a thing. But that said . . ."

"That said?"

"Mm . . . no, well . . . I see."

She almost never hesitated like that.

What could it mean?

"Watanuki."

"What?"

"I'd like some flowing somen."

". . . Huh?" He blinked.

"I want some flowing somen. Prepare it."

"Uh, um . . . now?"

"Yes. For dinner."

"Dinner . . . if you eat that for dinner at this time of year, it'll make the heat worse."

Which wasn't the point.

Kimihiro Watanuki was remarkably skilled at cooking and all kinds of housework. But flowing somen required an incredible amount of preparation. It was hardly the sort of thing that could be whipped up on short notice — out of the question.

"It shouldn't take that long. Just go cut a few stalks of bamboo grass on a nearby mountain."

"Or I could get a bamboo tree, so we could use it for Tanabata."

"My, my, Watanuki. So uneducated. Bamboo grass and bamboo have no clear difference, scientifically speaking. Much like eagles and hawks."

"Eagles and hawks aren't different?"

"Eagles are bigger than hawks. The names were given based on appearance, but they are actually the same thing."

"But even so, you couldn't use bamboo grass for flowing somen."

---

* *Flowing somen* See the notes for manga volume 7. Bamboo grass (*sasa*) is simply a young bamboo tree (*take*). *Tanabata* is a summer festival where people often write wishes on pieces of paper before tying them to bamboo.

"You could if you tried."

"I can't even imagine trying." You could only send a couple of noodles at a time, making the entire process even more involved.

"But I want to eat flowing somen. I want to eat it so, so bad! My body demands it!"

"Who are you, Yang Guifei? If you really insist, I might be able to get it ready for lunch tomorrow, Yûko-san. It's a Saturday, and that should be enough time for me to borrow some tools from friends."

"Knowing exactly what to do, despite all your complaints, is what makes Watanuki Watanuki."

This proof of identity he found particularly ominous. If a shape-changing enemy appeared, they would have to prove which of them was the real Kimihiro Watanuki based on each one's ability to acquire the implements for preparing flowing somen . . .

Which would suck.

"Lunch tomorrow . . . that will try my patience. If I am forced to eat something besides flowing somen today, I may well die."

"Glad to hear it. . . . Pretend I didn't say that."

"Mm-hmm."

"Anyway, tonight's menu is already set. We're having curry soup. You told me to make that, so I picked up the ingredients on the way here from the hospital—"

---

* *Yang Guifei* Known in Japan as *Youkihi*. One of the four beauties of ancient China, she was the concubine of Tang Dynasty Emperor Xuanzong. She was known for outrageous culinary demands, and had an entire network of horsemen set up for no other reason than to bring her lychee. She apparently hung herself after her family was blamed for a rebellion, but there are legends in Japan that she escaped there instead.

"Watanuki."

Then . . .

. . . Yûko asked the question.

"Can you understand the feelings of people who are unable to accept everyday happiness?"

"Huh?"

"For example . . . if someone won three hundred million yen in the lottery, but never claimed the prize . . . could you understand their feelings?"

"Umm . . . no, not really."

If you win the lottery, you take the money.

Stands to reason.

"I mean . . . that's what you would call a 'fair price,' isn't it?" he said.

"It is. The airs you give yourself are most unpleasant, but you are absolutely correct. Let me try another example. Imagine Himawari-chan tells Watanuki she loves him. What would you do?"

"Wh-what would I . . . ?"

Himawari-chan was Himawari Kunogi, Kimihiro Watanuki's classmate at Cross Private School.

A very, very cute girl.

"No, I mean . . . Yûko-san, that would . . . out of the blue like that I just can't . . ."

"Oh? You'd turn her down?"

"God no! O-obviously, I'd be thrilled!"

"Mm." Yûko nodded, narrowing her eyes. "That is because you are capable of accepting happiness."

"Happiness?"

"That's why you don't understand how she feels."

". . . . ."

"How Nurie Kushimura feels."

That . . . was true.

Watanuki had been able to understand the facts of what Nurie Kushimura had told him, but . . . if he were honest, none of it made any sense to him.

Not really.

He did not understand her.

He even found her unsettling.

Self-destruction, self-destructive tendencies, self-inflicted injuries.

For no reason at all—or, simply to violate taboos.

"She can't . . . accept happiness."

Was that feeling even human?

He wasn't completely immune to the impulse to do things that were forbidden; as she said, everyone could understand the desire to push the button marked DON'T PUSH.

But . . . rejecting happiness was different.

Put another way, it was like deliberately throwing yourself into unhappiness.

Flinging yourself into oncoming traffic.

Telling someone you love that you hate them.

Telling someone you hate that you love them.

Behaving in such a way . . .

. . . was not normal.

It was not what humans did.

———

Which meant . . . spirits.

———

At this point Yûko-san peeled herself away from the sofa, where she had been sprawled regally, and placed her pipe aside.

And . . .

Brushed her long hair back so she could put on the fake glasses.

They were cheap things, only 105 yen, but . . .

When Yûko Ichihara wore them, they were incredibly becoming.

In a manner of speaking.

"Very well. Watanuki, bring her to me."

"Huh? Who?"

"That woman. Bring her here."

Here.

To the shop that granted wishes.

"Er . . . no, but she's still in the hospital . . ."

"But she's not seriously injured. Just a fracture in one arm. There shouldn't be a problem with her slipping out for an hour."

"Well . . ."

She was right.

Still, he wasn't sure.

After all . . . it would require a payment.

"Whether you bring her or not, the results will be the same. My shop is everywhere and nowhere. If there is a thread leading here, anyone can enter from anywhere, and if they have entered, then they have sufficient *hitsuzen* to have done so."

"*. . . Hitsuzen.*"

"*Hitsuzen,*" she said again. "If this one succumbed to her 'urges' in front of you, then that is a thread, that is *hitsuzen*. If you don't bring her here, I will simply have to go to her."

* *Hitsuzen* Inevitability.

"More pushy sales?"

"*Hitsuzen!*" Yûko answered, smoothly. "If you ever say that again, I will halve your wages. Do you hear me?"

"Yes, but if you did that, I would definitely quit."

"Oh dear. If you quit, I will have no idea what to eat anymore. Let me withdraw it. If you press the point any further, I will turn you into a pressed flower."

A pressed flower?

Would she flatten him between the pages of a book?

"I'd rather you halved my wages."

"Oh? I shall remember that. At any rate, this case should be a good experience for you."

"A good experience?"

"Yes."

"You mean . . ."

A case like this?

What kind of case was it?

"Watanuki, surely you haven't forgotten why you're working here?" she said, taking off the glasses. She came over to Watanuki and put them in his hand.

He wondered why.

"Put them away somewhere," she said, airily.

Done playing with them already?

He'd spent more on train fare than on the glasses. This just drove home what a waste of effort it had been.

What *was* he working here for?

---

* *Pressed flower*   Not as much a non sequitur as it might seem. The term for "pushy sales" is *oshi-uri*, while "pressed flower" is *oshibana*. The first character is the same in both phrases.

"Right. Let's have that curry soup," Yûko said.

With an innocent grin.

■　■　■　■

I couldn't accept happiness?

Watanuki had hesitantly asked me whether this was so.

"Happiness?" The question flustered me.

Not because I didn't know what he meant, but because those words had gone right to the source of me.

They were . . .

. . . too accurate.

"Th-that's just . . . so sudden. I . . ." I found myself babbling, trying to cover.

"Mm . . ." Watanuki didn't seem very confident in his own words. "Yeah," he said, scratching his head awkwardly.

Watching me.

Or, no . . .

. . . watching my shoulder.

Weird. It was as if . . . he could see something.

Like he was trying to see something.

Was something there?

I glanced down at my shoulder . . . but of course, there was nothing there. How could there be? How could there be anything on my shoulder without me knowing?

On my shoulder . . .

Was it the left or the right shoulder that ghosts attached themselves to?

Yeah, right.

"I just meant . . . a normal life, normal happiness . . . can you accept that as it comes to you?"

Watanuki-kun tried explaining it a different way. But he was saying the same thing — like a junior high school student whose class presentation consisted only of repeating the contents of a book he'd borrowed from the library. He said the words without knowing what they meant.

Words he'd been given by someone else.

I thought.

". . . Yes," I said nodding.

The day before . . .

This boy, Kimihiro Watanuki, had come to visit. Apparently he had been standing behind me when I jumped out into traffic. He was there for shopping, or work, or both. That's probably why he looked familiar. Such an adorable face that it had stayed with me. I remembered hardly anything leading up to the accident, but I did remember him; human memory is the strangest thing.

But he was quite a busybody.

He had called an ambulance . . . which was, well, normal enough; doing that was increasingly rare these days, but not out of the question. But for a complete stranger, a random passerby, to be concerned enough to come visit with flowers in hand was sort of alarming.

Was he just being nice?

Perhaps he was just nosy.

I would never have done anything like that. At most, after being hit by a car I might have taken a picture of myself with my cell phone camera and sent it around to my friends.

Mean as that would be.

After all, I would have deserved it.

I was the one who had jumped out into traffic.

———

Even though I knew I would get run over.

———

I knew that perfectly well.

Which meant he was nice.

Alarmingly nice.

What drove Watanuki-kun to involve himself, of his own free will, with someone who was obviously bad news? With someone like me? When he had visited yesterday, I had merely thought he was unusually nice, but . . . here he was again. Despite the way I had treated him, he had come a second time.

Sure, I had apologized, and Watanuki-kun had forgiven me.

Was he a masochist?

He did appear to be a rather unfortunate boy. Unlucky in love, very few friends, bullied by his boss . . . If all that were true, it might explain the look in his eyes.

"Weird . . . I feel like someone is thinking very rude thoughts about me. Must be Yûko-san," Watanuki muttered, looking around.

Good instincts.

But who was Yûko-san?

"Or maybe Dômeki? Curse you, Dômeki! Ahem . . . anyway. Kushimura-san, yesterday you told me quite a lot of things that made me think, and the more I thought about it . . . it all just seems very odd."

Odd.

She knew that. Without him pointing it out.

"So . . . don't you want to do something about it?" He looked at me.

"Do . . . ?"

"I mean, it's not good for you. This time you were lucky enough to get off with a fracture, but if you keep doing this sort of thing . . ."

"Keep doing like I've been doing? Walking hand in hand with those inexplicable, inarguable urges? It baffles me too. A complete mystery. Do I have no interest in my own happiness? That might well be true. I've never . . . been very aggressive in the pursuit of happiness."

Apparently the pursuit of happiness was a right everyone in Japan possessed, guaranteed to us in the constitution. Which meant I was waiving that right. And not only waiving it—trampling it.

Even denying my own right to life.

Even though I didn't want to die.

"Wanting to do things you're told not to do . . . a very childish way of putting it, but that very childishness makes it easy to understand. It's the simplest way I can explain it. Watanuki-kun, haven't you felt like that yourself? Even at your age?"

"Well . . . I guess I understand, but when I hear you talk . . . I find it hard to believe what *you* feel is just an extension of what *I* do. To me it feels like you jumped the tracks ages back."

Jumped the tracks.

This time it was his own words; there was a real confidence to them. And once again . . . he was right.

Getting right to the root of the matter.

"I must seem so ugly," I said.

". . . . . . . ugly?"

"I'm so different from . . . normal people. It must make them sick to look at me."

". . . sick?"

"Yes. Just like you said, Watanuki-kun. I was trying to generalize the problem by saying that everyone has the urges I do . . . but that's not really true."

I knew that.

I'd insisted I was normal, perfectly normal, to the point of genuine weirdness—which had just made my condition worse. I had been so reluctant to let go of that connection to normal, to what was ordinary.

No matter how far from the tracks I got, I wanted to believe our roots were the same.

Finally I said, "Not being able to accept happiness . . . that is odd, isn't it? But I'll just go on like this, I'll just keep making trouble for people around me. Maybe it would have been better . . . the day before yesterday, if I'd hit my head and died. . . ."

"Absolutely not!" Watanuki-kun roared, suddenly furious.

His appearance had been so gentle that I had never dreamed my attitude would enrage him like this. I bit back the next words.

I didn't say it would be better if I *was* dead.

"P-probably . . . none of this is your fault, Kushimura-san! Something bad has taken hold of you, and it is causing you to make the wrong decisions where it matters most! I'm told there are things that can do that! Which means none of it is your fault!"

"Taken . . . hold of me?" A dramatic way of putting things.

Despite myself, I glanced at my shoulder again.

Which shoulder was it where the ghosts took hold of you?

"Wrong decisions . . . wrong choices . . . I mean, trying to be happy is just normal! Pushing happiness away . . . that just doesn't make sense!"

"Y-yeah . . ."

Honestly, I nodded here not because I agreed with him, but because I was bowled over by his force, his earnestness. My head bobbed before I could think to stop it.

But.

I knew this boy was happy.

People who pushed happiness away didn't make sense to him. He couldn't believe that anyone could be like that; it had no connection with the world as he knew it. Which meant the world he lived in must be overflowing with happiness.

So much for him being unfortunate.

I was actually a little jealous.

Oh.

I could feel another urge coming on.

Watanuki-kun had said all this for me, yet I found myself wondering what would happen if I got mad at him—I couldn't think of any logical reasons to refute what he said, so I would just have to reject his goodwill as forcefully as possible.

Maybe even slap him.

What would he do then?

Someone this nice—what would he do?

Someone this happy.

I wrapped my free arm tightly around myself. Watanuki-kun noticed that immediately, and must have assumed my condition had taken a turn for the worse, because he asked kindly if I was feeling all right.

Oh no—I didn't think I could resist this urge.

Watanuki-kun reached for the nurse call button.

The nurse call . . .

Since I woke up I had pushed it for no reason so many times, all day, all night. Because it was a button I should not be pushing. A button I should be pushing only in emergencies. Which meant I wanted to push it all the time. The nurses had been very angry with me, and if Watanuki-kun pushed the button, I was sure they would assume it was another prank.

Even though it wasn't a prank.

Even though it wasn't a prank.

If I slapped this boy hard enough to knock his glasses off . . .

I didn't want to do that.

I didn't.

I didn't. I didn't. I didn't. I didn't. I didn't. I didn't. I didn't. I didn't. I didn't. I didn't. I didn't. I didn't. I didn't. I didn't. I didn't. I didn't. I didn't. I didn't. I didn't. I didn't.

I didn't, but I couldn't—

"Look at me!" Watanuki-kun said, quite loudly.

That was just enough to bring me back to myself.

But it was not enough.

He had to leave. I couldn't stop myself a second time.

"Uh, um . . . Kushimura-san," Watanuki-kun said, before I could work out how to ask him to leave without being breathtakingly rude. "There's someone I think you should meet . . ."

And an hour later . . .

I was in that shop.

The shop that could grant any wish.

■ ■ ■ ■

Describing the situation with such a clichéd expression may fail to communicate the exact meaning of the scene, but allow me to use it anyway—it was like a snake and a frog staring each other down. No matter how grimly both parties were glaring, to the independent observer the eventual victor was a foregone conclusion.

Yûko Ichihara and Nurie Kushimura.

Yûko Ichihara sprawled languidly like arrogance given clothes, while the tiny Nurie Kushimura failed to project anything like confidence, and was unable even to meet her opponent's gaze. They were opposites, images reflected in a mirror.

Kimihiro Watanuki observed their interaction from the next room, peering through the crack in the screens. He had brought Kushimura to the shop that could grant any wish, brought her inside, prepared coffee for her and Yûko, and had left the room since his presence did not seem particularly welcome. But he had been unable to restrain his curiosity, which was why he was hunched over like a Peeping Tom.

His role was completed.

If *hitsuzen* had been at work, then it had ended where Watanuki was concerned the moment he brought Kushimura here.

Which had been difficult enough.

But today she had not hit him with flowers—largely because he had known she would overreact if he brought anything with him and so had gone empty-handed, rude as that might seem—or done anything else out of the ordinary, so his difficulties had resided entirely in the effort it took to persuade her to see Yûko Ichihara.

But it had not been all that difficult.

He had done as Yûko instructed—explained the proposal with reluctance, hinted strongly that he did not personally recommend it and that the risk involved was fairly high—and indeed, with shocking ease Kushimura was firmly demanding that he take her to the shop.

When Yûko had told him to present things in that way, Watanuki had had no idea what she meant, but once he saw it in action it was obvious. Her instructions had played on Kushimura's urges to violate taboo to get her to do exactly what Yûko wanted.

This was not the first time he'd seen her pull off something similar. Yûko Ichihara was as cunning as they came.

But . . .

When he had been hinting that he did not recommend it, and that there was risk involved, Watanuki had not been lying. He had not tricked Kushimura.

Both those things were true, in his opinion.

Just how great a "fair price" would Yûko Ichihara demand from Nurie Kushimura? To solve her worries, to grant her wish, how much would Kushimura give up?

Concern getting the better of curiosity—indeed, throwing it right through the saloon doors of his mind—Watanuki gulped as he watched Yûko and Kushimura interact, although all they had done so far was give their respective names (and Kushimura had been forced to give her birthday). Neither one seemed inclined to say anything further. Nor did either of them show any signs of drinking the coffee Watanuki had prepared. He had even gone to the trouble of warming up the cups, so he would definitely have preferred them to drink it hot.

Then . . . at last Kushimura reached for her coffee.

. . .

"Call me Yûko," Yûko abruptly said. "And—that thing you were about to do? Don't."

Kushimura looked up, surprised.

Yûko smiled faintly. "Or perhaps . . . *this* way of putting things would work better with you, Nurie Kushimura-san.

"Go ahead. I dare you."

"Eh? Uh, um . . ." Kushimura spluttered, obviously taken aback by what must have made little sense to her. Already Yûko had taken control of the conversation, Watanuki thought. He waited breathlessly, wondering if Kushimura would be able to keep up. "I—I don't know . . ."

"What I mean? Sure," Yûko spat.

Maintaining superiority.

Watanuki had explained Yûko to Kushimura as a sort of counselor, which seemed the most easily acceptable way of describing what went on in Yûko's shop. Her haughty manner must have come as a bit of a surprise.

"So, what exactly do you want from me?" his employer continued.

"Eh . . . um, I just . . . followed Watanuki here," Kushimura explained, in a very small voice. The end of each phrase trailed off so quietly that Watanuki was unable to overhear.

"This is the shop where wishes are granted. Where all wishes come true. If you have entered this shop, if you have been led to this shop, then you must have a wish you long to have granted. Whether you are consciously aware of it or not."

". . . any wish?"

"Of course. Any wish at all."

"Um . . . I'm not . . . exactly normal. Is that a problem?"

"Absolutely not."

If a fair price was paid, Yûko added.

To Kimihiro Watanuki's eyes and senses, Nurie Kushimura's wish had grown quite desperate—her life depended on it. Which meant the price she would have to pay . . . might well involve her soul.

That would square things.

But even so, even with that in mind . . .

Yûko had called this case a good experience.

"I want . . ." Kushimura said. There was a brief silence.

"I want . . . to stop myself."

"Stop yourself?" Yûko echoed deliberately.

"Yes. I want . . . . to stop myself."

Stop herself . . . from doing what she did not want to do. That was her wish.

"I believe you already are."

"Huh?"

"Never mind. So, if that is your wish, what is it, specifically, that you wish to stop yourself from doing?"

Kushimura started to answer, then hung her head. She seemed to be choosing her words carefully, but what eventually came out was exactly what she'd said to Watanuki.

"My urges," she said. "I have these urges that make me want to violate taboos."

"To push buttons marked 'DON'T PUSH'?"

"Y-yes. Exactly."

"You can't accept happiness," Yûko said, looking directly at Watanuki.

She was well aware that he was watching. But she soon turned her gaze back to Kushimura.

"For example, if you bought a lottery ticket, and won three hundred million yen . . . what would you do?"

"What would I . . . ?"

"Would you claim the prize?"

"Well . . ." Kushimura hesitated, made a show of mulling it over, and then answered with what she had most probably known instantly. "No, I don't think I would."

Watanuki had known how she would answer.

But he could not accept it.

He thought Yûko would ask why not, follow up on the question, but instead she just said,

"I see."

She seemed oddly uninterested in Kushimura, to the point where Watanuki longed to say something.

Putting aside issues of customer service—even putting aside the fact that Yûko herself had ordered Watanuki to bring Kushimura here—this was hardly a way to treat an injured woman, a woman with her arm in a sling. Not that Yûko was the type to care about any of that.

"I-I've been like this since I was a child. Every time I saw the right way to do things, the better path to follow . . . I found myself doing something else, messing everything up . . . just like I knew I would."

Since Yûko refused to say anything, Kushimura seemed

to be forcing herself to talk, trying to cover the awkward silence.

"I don't have any real reason to wish I was dead, but I've done things that look suicidal. It's like when something good happens I want to die, when I'm happy I want to be unhappy. Um, Ichiha . . . Yûko-san, do you know what I mean? Do you ever feel like I do?"

"No and never," Yûko snapped. "Those feelings belong to you."

Kushimura said nothing.

"I don't know how you feel about them, but they are your feelings and your thoughts," Yûko went on. "If you agree with them, if you believe them to be the right thing, then that is what they are."

There's no reason to stop yourself, Yûko said.

"Every human being thinks different things are right, and different things are wrong. Whether something is normal or not, it is still different for every person. Happiness is the same—everyone has their own definition of it. Do you still want to stop yourself? Stop those feelings you call your urges?"

"O-of course. This is all . . . all so odd. I'm causing problems for everyone, and . . . these injuries . . ."

"I heard about that from my Watanuki."

My Watanuki?

"You heard . . . ?"

"That boy loves to gossip."

Now she was spreading rumors about him.

"But how much is true? You say you're causing problems for everyone, but to what degree are you including yourself in 'everyone'?"

"M-myself?"

"Everyone finds happiness differently, but ultimately, happiness is a bargain with yourself," Yûko said.

"A b-bargain?"

"A promise to yourself."

This . . .

. . . Watanuki had heard before.

And he knew what followed.

"You need two things: action and sincerity. Effort must be rewarded. If you pile hardship upon hardship, overcome difficulty after difficulty and give yourself nothing in return, you violate your contract."

"Violate . . . my contract."

"And how can that be anything but insincere?"

Yûko seemed to be enjoying herself immensely, inappropriately.

"You are betraying yourself. And not only betraying, but cutting the thread."

The thread.

Hitsuzen.

"I'm sure our boy told you there are no people who reject happiness . . . or something similarly naive."

He had.

But how did she know?

"But calling him naive hardly covers it. Being happy is not a right, but a duty. A duty to yourself. Waiving rights is one thing, but failing in your duty is downright irresponsible."

Insincere—and irresponsible.

Which meant that behavior was also taboo.

"If you win the lottery, you should claim the prize. That is what I call fair price. You should pay ten thousand yen for something worth ten thousand yen and you should be paid three hundred million yen for something worth three hundred million yen. Discounts and bargains simply upset the balance."

As she said the word "balance," Yûko inclined her head upward and clapped twice. Watanuki could not work out what this gesture meant, and did nothing. Yûko clapped again. Twice.

"Where are you?" she snapped, clapping a third time.

Is she calling me? What am I, some sort of ninja? She wants me to appear from the rafters? Appalled questions flooded through Watanuki's mind as he silently opened the screen.

"At your service," he said, stepping into the room.

Responding appropriately, despite himself.

Yûko had been well aware that he was watching, but apparently Kushimura had not been, and she gave a sigh of relief when she saw him. Being alone with Yûko must have been extremely stressful for her.

It seemed so.

"Watanuki, bring the item," Yûko said, haughtily.

As if addressing one of her minions.

"The item?"

"The item you obtained the other day at the shop where items of little value gather."

". . . . . ?"

---

* *Ninja*   Cheesy samurai dramas often had ninja hiding in the rafters, waiting to be summoned by a clap of their employer's hands.

He almost insisted that he had never been to such a fantastic-sounding place, but before he did, it occurred to him that she must mean the hundred-yen shop.

Such a poetic description.

"Hurry!" Yûko said, in a tone that did not allow for argument.

Watanuki nodded awkwardly, and left the room.

If *the shop where items of little value gather* meant the hundred-yen shop, then *the item* must mean the fake glasses. He had been told to put them away somewhere, so he had . . . but where? Oh, right, certain they would never be used again, he had put them in the storage shed out back. The shed . . . which Yûko called the treasury.

Her mountain of treasure.

When he first heard this, Watanuki had secretly pitied her inability to distinguish between treasures and junk, but certain events since then had caused him to reconsider. He had his doubts about how much of it qualified as treasure, but it did seem to be true that much of what lay inside was decidedly not normal.

He found the fake glasses quickly, then went back to the room and gave them to Yûko.

Without so much as a glance in his direction, let alone a word of thanks, Yûko turned toward Kushimura. "These glasses have quite a distinguished history."

Yeah, a very distinguished hundred-yen shop.

"If you wear these regularly, a mysterious power will lead you down the right path. They will prevent you from making the wrong choices. They will show you how to select the behavior that will help you become as you see yourself, to do what is best for you."

"Th-they will?" Kushimura was dubious, but unable to take her eyes off the glasses. Was she really going to believe vague talk about mysterious powers? "Those are . . . some very impressive glasses."

"They have been linked to Date Masamune."

For some reason, Yûko was adding extra unneeded lies. It made Watanuki's knees tremble just to listen.

"I now give them to you," Yûko said, reverently handing to Kushimura the distinguished item that had been linked to Date Masamune. Kushimura took them, but she did seem sure what to do with them. She grasped them awkwardly by the frames and held them up near her eyes.

"But I have good eyes . . ."

"The lenses aren't curved at all, don't worry."

"Oh, I see . . . but I don't have much money . . ."

"They're free," Yûko said. "That's what 'give' implies."

Kushimura nodded. Watanuki, however, was flabbergasted. "Give?" Yûko-san? "Free?" No fair price at all?

"You are 'free' to do with them what you like. Use them, throw them away, as you like. Decide however action and sincerity dictate. Now, shouldn't you be getting back to the hospital? You slipped out without permission, didn't you? You can find your own way back, I'm sure. I would love to have our boy walk you back, but he has important work to do."

"Ah . . . right, yes, I'll be fine. I can get back, I'm sure. Umm . . . thank you."

A very uncertain expression of gratitude.

As well it should be; if she left here, she would only wonder why she had come. There was not one single reason why she should be thanking anybody. Nothing had been done for her, and she had done nothing. At the very end, she had been given a highly dubious pair of fake glasses. Given? More like forced to accept. And then sent packing.

But once Yûko had wrapped things up, there was nothing more to say.

That much was perfectly clear.

Without a drop of the coffee Watanuki had prepared passing her lips.

———

Kushimura left the shop where wishes were granted.

———

Watanuki did walk her to the gate, considering it the least he could do.

When he returned to Yûko, she was puffing on her pipe.

Had she refrained from doing so as some small consideration for her injured guest?

That did not seem likely.

"What was that all about?"

"What was what about?" Yûko said, blankly.

"Where do I even start? Um ... first of all, the fake glasses?"

"What about them? They are undoubtedly an item of distinguishment, and they are undoubtedly linked to Date Masamune."

"Date Masamune has nothing to do with them."

"You cannot deny the possibility exists."

"I believe I can," Watanuki insisted. "And the rest of what you said to her, about how they would help her choose the right path ... That was all nonsense, right?"

"Oh? You noticed?"

"Fake glasses that cost a hundred and five yen the other day do not simply acquire such properties overnight."

"That is not necessarily true, but in this case, yes, those glasses are perfectly ordinary glasses."

Without so much as batting an eye, Yûko admitted that they had no effect at all.

"I thought as much. You would never hand over something that impressive without demanding a fair price."

"I don't much like your tone, but for the moment I'll agree. Nevertheless, Watanuki, that perception of yours is not quite accurate."

"Oh?"

"I did receive a fair price from her," Yûko said. "And her wish was granted."

". . . how so?"

But Yûko just smiled.

Regally.

"To further the example from yesterday: If an English gentleman came up to you on your way home from school and said, 'I'd like to give you one hundred trillion yen.' Perhaps he says this in Japanese, perhaps in English, it does not really matter—if that happened, Watanuki, what would you do?"

"I-I'm not . . ."

"Would you take it or not?"

"Well . . ." He couldn't answer.

But this was the sort of question that not being able to answer instantly was in itself the answer.

"Well, no. I wouldn't."

"Why not?"

"I mean, that just sounds so suspicious. He must be up to something."

"I see," Yûko nodded. "Exactly my point."

"Said point being?"

"That is the best way to explain people who can't accept happiness. I gave no indication that this English gentleman was up to anything—and English gentlemen are the most honorable gentlemen in the world. They would never be up to anything suspicious."

"I have no idea what inspired such deep-seated trust in you, but a figure like a hundred trillion yen would make anyone suspicious."

"That's a comment I would have liked to hear in the 'Himawari-chan tells you she loves you' hypothetical. But essentially, the opposite of what I said to her."

The opposite.

Looked at from the other direction.

Yûko went on. "To become happy, you need to pay a fair price. Which means that excessive fortune can only be viewed as a threat. You need to *earn* that fortune through an appropriate amount of work and struggle."

"A contract with yourself?"

A promise to yourself.

Action and sincerity.

"You know the expression 'It all works out in the end'? Human lives ultimately run on a balanced budget. If there is good, there is bad, and when bad things happen there must be good things as well."

"That . . ."

That would square things.

". . . I have heard that."

"But the expression is not strictly accurate. Fundamentally, to be happy you have to bear the burden of an equal amount of misery. See? To get something good, you have to put up with something bad. Nothing as carefree as 'taking the good with the bad' makes it sound. That doesn't fulfill the promise."

Watanuki thought about it. Yuko went on:

"To put it another way, the higher your position at a job, the more you have to work. Not being able to do so is insincere and irresponsible. Still another way: If where you are is a step lower than normal, if you are in an unfortunate position, then you must allow yourself to *not* expend as much effort, to abandon your stubborn pride. All part of the promise."

"But . . . um . . ."

Was this true?

He could comprehend the gist of what she was saying, but . . .

"B-but she—Kushimura-san, Nurie Kushimura-san, in her case—she didn't have excessive happiness, she was abandoning normal happiness."

Waiving her rights and abandoning her duties.

"She was not, Watanuki," Yûko said reproachfully. "She was maintaining her balance."

"Balance?"

"All humans have a certain level of fascination with forbidden behavior, but those urges have little to do with Kushimura's situation. You must not mingle or confuse the two. All that I have just explained ought to have been enough for you to understand that happiness, excessive or otherwise, carries with it a degree of pressure. Happiness is not entirely a good thing—not as long as you have to pay a fair price for it. And there is no way to avoid paying the price."

"Huh . . ."

If you accepted the hundred trillion yen from the English gentleman, you would have to work off a hundred trillion yen's worth of debt to yourself.

The debt would be *hitsuzen.*

Not to the English gentleman—but to yourself.

"When she was with me, the only thought in her mind was that she wanted to go home. Talking with me was a source of pressure. That's why she was so relieved when you came in."

"Yeah, I did notice that . . ."

"In return for abandoning happiness, she can escape that pressure. She made that choice. Just as she said, this is not self-destructive or suicidal; it was all carefully calculated."

"C-calculated?"

Calculated, measured, weighed.

Not the hallmarks of impulsive behavior.

"In other words, she was an immense coward about getting what she wanted most."

"B-but . . . you don't think she was simply throwing herself at unhappiness? Even if that was less stressful."

"Throwing herself into unhappiness . . . or into traffic?"

"Yeah, like that."

"But she was hit by a scooter," Yûko said, dismissively. "She chose when to jump. And jumping out in front of a dump truck is a much bigger taboo."

If she were hit by a scooter . . . she would not die. Especially if she blocked it with her arm. It made sense; Kushimura had chosen when to jump out in traffic, and had chosen to jump in front of the scooter.

"As a result of which, she did not have to give a major presentation at work. She was able to avoid such a stressful situation, to avoid that pressure."

"Yeah, but . . ."

"And while she claimed she caused trouble for everyone, it wasn't actually that big a deal. Someone filled in for her . . . what was his name? Hyôdô-kun? He did her job for her, and whether she was there or not, she was still part of the group that had made the plan, and no matter what she might say, the road to promotion is not as firmly closed as she claims."

"Well . . . I guess not."

No guess about it.

That was it, plain and simple.

"Or maybe she simply didn't want that promotion. Truly meek people fear success more than failure. Promotions bring with them greater responsibility, and there are any number of people who would prefer to avoid that. For all her concerns about causing trouble for her group, she also admitted that they were all really nice people. And she knew that better than anyone."

"But . . . she hit me with those flowers . . ."

"A visitor so Sewashi-kun-ish—abnormally nice and so eager to be helpful that he calls an ambulance for a total stranger—is hardly likely to be particularly enraged when the injured person they are visiting hits them over the head with a bouquet. Admittedly, she did so without knowing that you are prone to violent fits."

"I am not!"

There were just people near him who set him off. Two of them.

And one of them was right in front of him.

"If you think about it, annoying the nurses by pressing the button that summons them over and over is not that big a deal. Same with the fire alarm at school. That button marked 'DON'T PUSH' is hardly the launch switch for a nuclear bomb. I'm sure she got off with a scolding. Perhaps that's what she's after: anything except happiness, including making people angry. Like ordering coffee when you want tea. Speaking of which, she almost threw her coffee at me."

She had?

So that's what Yûko had stopped her from doing.

"She had calculated that I knew her situation and was going to help with it, so I would not be all that angry."

Watanuki was silent.

"The old idea that things are going too well. Watanuki, can you understand the desire to stumble deliberately when the story looks to progress your way? 'Trouble follows fortune.' So why not trip yourself up in advance? If you're going be tripped anyway, trip yourself before anything good happens. I have no idea how conscious she is of what she's doing, but it is, to a certain extent, deliberate."

"Oh . . ."

Were there really people like that?

Someone that thorough.

"She mentioned failing to get into the schools she most wanted to attend, but she always got in somewhere else. She may have failed to get the job she wanted most, but she was hired by her second choice. She mentioned fighting the urge to throw herself in front of the train at the station . . . but she never actually did."

The most she ever did was jump out in front of a scooter that was slowing down as it approached a crosswalk.

"And when you get right down to it, the fact that she is alive now proves everything. The fact that she has survived this long is not a miracle, it is proof. The greatest taboo for a human is suicide. If you're satisfied by pretending to kill yourself, then the action cannot be taken as a violation of that taboo."

She had cut her wrists once—but only once. And the cuts had been too shallow to kill her.

"If there was a button marked 'DON'T PUSH,' that woman would never push it," Yuko went on. "She would just claim she would, and convince herself that it was true. In that sense, she's wrong about herself. She's never killed anyone, she's never eaten anybody, yet she talks about violating taboos? Makes my sides hurt laughing. Any number of children have jumped out the window of their classroom. That's not a taboo! Look at it all lined up like this, Watanuki, and you can tell just how calculating that woman is."

Avoiding happiness.

Avoiding pressure.

"A word as forthright and flamboyant as 'urges' hardly describes such a slipshod methodology. What she does is simply a compromise. It seems you are not among them, Watanuki, but there are any number of people who do not like being exalted, do not like being thought highly of, and the vast majority of those people invariably choose the second-best option."

The second-best option.

"A problem of balance and swift adjustment. Nobody can afford to keep the gas pedal down all the time, can they? You'd never make it around the next corner. You could boil it down to overcautiousness, or underestimating oneself, but either way, refusing to accept a normal amount of happiness can hardly be described as the right thing to do."

"The right thing to do?"

"It is your duty to accept a measure of happiness equivalent to the actions you have taken. Rejecting it violates your contract with yourself. If your effort is not rewarded, your soul rebels."

"Rebels . . ."

"You could also say it overflows. If you do the work to receive the best option, then you must accept that option as your reward."

That was the fair price.

A fair price could neither be undercut nor overpaid.

Yûko pointed her pipe at the seat where Kushimura had been a few minutes before.

"Stop herself from doing what she doesn't want to do . . . a fascinating turn of phrase, and one that makes no sense. The fact that she doesn't want to do those things suggests she is already stopping herself from doing them—very calculatedly. She may well have a black belt in stopping herself. Never once leaving the realm of safety, never even going close to the fence around the realm. The only question is, to what extent is she herself aware of this?"

---

* *Overflows* The word used for "rebellion" or "revolt" is a homonym of the word for "flood" or "overflow." Both words are read *hanran*.

". . . If she puts those glasses on," Watanuki said, trying to hide how shaken he was, "will she really . . . be able to choose the path that's best for her?"

"Of course not," Yûko said, as if it were obvious. "Those are an ordinary pair of fake glasses."

"Eh . . . but . . . then . . ."

"Watanuki, you said it yourself. Have you already forgotten how pompously you lectured me for deceiving her? You must be suffering from amnesia."

"No, I mean, you're right, but . . . then what was the point of it all?"

"There is a point . . . just not a dramatic one."

Watanuki waited.

"I merely provided an opportunity."

She had not become any more involved than that.

"Watanuki, you always wear glasses. But if you were to take them off, do you think you wouldn't be able to see spirits anymore?"

"Huh?"

"Or if you close your eyes. That would prevent you from seeing them. Even more extreme—you could gouge both eyes out. Would that get rid of the spirits that gather around you?"

"Now you're starting to scare me," Watanuki said, backing away from Yûko and protecting his eyes.

"I exist to scare you. Answer the question. If that would work, you would hardly need to continue your life of indentured servitude here."

"Nah, nothing like that would really solve the problem. Spirits aren't there because I can see them; I can see them because they're there. As long as they're attracted by my blood, I'm sure I'll still be able to sense them."

And that . . .

. . . meant that not only his sight, but all five of his senses, and his sixth sense as well, would have to be shut down. Or nothing would change.

"Hmm, you think not?"

"Well . . . I've never tried, so I don't know for sure."

"Want to?"

"Since the procedure would be irreversible, hell no!"

And if it failed, where would he be?

Watanuki was no adventure seeker.

"That's why the glasses themselves are of no importance," Yûko said, getting back to the point. "For someone without any vision problems, glasses are something unnatural, that is always in their line of sight, and they naturally focus on them. That's what makes my curse effective."

"Huh? Yûko-san, did you say curse?"

"I did not."

"You did so! You said it makes your curse effective! I heard you!"

"I said it makes my neurosis effective."

"In accomplishing *what*!?"

How could a neurosis be effective?

He couldn't begin to guess.

"She knew what was the best option without it being pointed out to her. She was avoiding it precisely *because* she

---

* *Neurosis* Untranslatable pun. "Curse" is *noroi*, "neurosis" is *noiroze*. I played around with using "spell" and "spelling," but ended up deciding that keeping the word as "curse" was more important than awkwardly trying to make the pun work.

knew. So . . . if you look at it a different way, all I had to do was make conscious what was unconscious. As time passes, what was unconscious may well become part of her, which would grant her wish. People who always wear glasses apparently feel them to be part of the face. It should take a few months for that to happen . . . and it won't be easy."

"Won't it? Once you get used to them, it's not a big deal."

"I'm not talking about glasses," Yûko said, full of malevolence. "Nurie Kushimura has never experienced the happiness she deserves; she has been busy avoiding it. It's built up inside her."

"B-built up?" What was? Happiness?

"By 'built up' I mean like sedimentary deposits are built up, and by 'deposits' I mean mud. Despite that, she will be forced to harvest happiness—if she is physically up to the task. But there's nothing else she can do; she has to pay off the price she promised herself before the bill is settled. She won't be finished till the receipt is in her hand."

Watanuki looked blank.

"The fair price she paid for the loss of her escape routes was the escape routes themselves. No matter how much pressure she is under, she will not allow herself to run away. I can only imagine how ugly that must be."

"Ugly . . . ?"

"Ultimately, it's up to her what she does next. She might choose to change nothing and keep running up her tab. If she throws away the glasses, she will continue to live a life of second-best options, as she always has. That might not be happiness . . . but neither is it misery."

That was as much as Yûko would involve herself.

She might touch upon the cause, but never reach down to the root of it.

Yûko probably viewed her lack of involvement as only natural. She never questioned morality, never asked if someone was good or bad—that was her way. Yûko was neither good nor deserving of being called evil; she simply was. Someone in her position had to maintain those standards, or she would eventually find herself thoroughly taken advantage of.

And presumably, she did not want that.

"Enough work! All done for the day! Ah, so draining! Watanuki, the coffee's gone cold, so make some more? Don't forget the milk and sugar."

"Okay, then . . . mm? W-wait, Yûko-san . . . ?"

"What? I'm not giving you a raise."

"I don't mean that . . ."

"What? I'm not giving you a *raise.*"

Don't say it in italics, Watanuki thought. Makes it feel unpleasantly *real.*

"You mean Kushimura-san's urges were her own problem, a problem entirely related to her contract with herself . . . and nothing to do with spirits at all?"

"Exactly," Yûko said, rolling her eyes, as if this had been covered hours ago. "You couldn't see anything, could you?"

"Well, no . . . but the first time? At the crosswalk, on her shoulder . . ."

"Something sewn on her shoulder bag that reflected the streetlights into your eyes?" Yûko said, giving him a bewitching smile.

That's why she had said . . .

"I told you this would be a good experience for you, didn't I? Remember that there are people like her."

"People like her . . . ?"

Nurie Kushimura.

Calculatedly avoiding happiness.

A "good experience" for him. Yuko had said that early on.

"Even without spirits getting involved, people can cause plenty of strange events on their own. You have a healthy mind, Watanuki, and there are all kinds of people you would consider creepy. That is part of mankind, something that dwells within all humans. You always talk about spirits as if they are frightening or evil, but there is nothing as frightening or evil as humans. When you have time, Watanuki, sit somewhere alone and toy with that idea awhile. When you have finished paying off your fair price, and your eyes can no longer see spirits . . .

———

"Will you be able to see people?"

———

He could have sworn . . .

. . . he heard the sound of horrible jagged teeth snapping shut.

"Just kidding!"

Watanuki was unable to respond.

Yûko continued merrily, "Now I'm all done with work, but you, Watanuki, have just begun! When my coffee is ready, you have quite a task ahead of you! You have to make up for being late yesterday and skipping entirely the day before, or you may find yourself working at this shop for all eternity!"

"What task?"

"Flowing somen!" Yûko beamed.

As if that was the best possible choice.

Good things always brought suffering.

■ ■ ■ ■

Oh.

Oh, no.

I did it again.

I wasted time.

And time is so precious.

Nobody could possibly solve my problems. Nobody could possibly grant my wish. I knew it would be pointless, so why?

Let that nice child talk me into it . . . let myself sit in that terrifying woman's gaze.

And all I got was this ordinary pair of glasses.

What was the point of that?

She had said things that sounded right, but anybody could tell these were cheaply made plastic things, the kind sold in any hundred-yen shop. The origins she had given were not remotely believable.

What was that all about?

Some sort of scam?

Taking advantage of people's troubles?

But it wasn't as though I'd lost anything. I had wasted a little time, but lost nothing. Not only that, but I had been given this pair of cheap fake glasses.

Fair price.

The boy had used that phrase.

But what fair price had I paid to acquire these? I didn't feel as though I had done anything, but now that I was thinking about it . . . something felt different.

Something felt wrong.

I felt as though I had lost a tangible part of myself.

Should I throw these things away?

These glasses . . . there was nothing special about them. If I threw them away, would this strange sense of loss inside me fade away?

As though I had lost a comfortable place.

As though I had lost a comfortable escape route.

As though I had a hole opened in my heart.

Or as though I had filled a hole in my heart.

I looked at the trash can.

I should throw these glasses in there.

But then . . .

———

"Go ahead. I dare you."

———

I heard her voice.

My hand stopped.

I was hearing things, of course. I had just remembered that phrase suddenly.

But . . . why not? I thought. I didn't need to make up my mind right away.

I walked on past the garbage can, keeping the glasses.

There was a crosswalk ahead of me.

The light was red, so I stopped.

I must be punished.
I must be punished.
I must be punished.
I must be punished.
I must be punished.
I must be punished.
I must be punished.
I must be punished.
I must be punished.
I must be punished.
I must be punished.
I must be punished.
I must be punished.
I must be punished.
I must be punished.
I must be punished.
I must be punished.
I must be punished.
I must be punished.
I must be punished.
I must be punished.
I must be punished.
I must be punished.
I must be punished.
I must be punished.
I must be punished.
I must be punished.
I must be punished.
I must be punished.
I must be punished.

I must be punished.
I must be punished.
I must be punished.
I must be punished.
I must be punished.
I must be punished.
I must be punished.
I must be punished.
I must be punished.
I must be punished.
I must be punished.
I must be punished.
I must be punished.
I must be punished.
I must be punished.
I must be punished.
I must be punished.
I must be punished.
I must be punished.
I must be punished.
I must be punished.
I must be punished.
I must be punished.
I must be punished.
I must be punished.
I must be punished.
I must be punished.
I must be punished.
I must be punished.
I must be punished.

Knnn knnn — my cell phone vibrating.

New message.
Addressed, of course, to me.
From, of course, my dead friend.
I must be punished.

■ ■ ■ ■

There are a great many strange things in the world.

But no matter how odd . . .
How incredible something may be . . .

If a human does not touch it . . .
If a human does not see it . . .
If a human is not involved with it . . .

It is simply a phenomenon.
Simply a matter that will fade with time.

Humans.
Mankind.
Homo sapiens.

Humans are the most profoundly mysterious living things in
the world!

■ ■ ■ ■

How many people know the pain of being born on April 1? Their tragic lot is not widely understood. The more perceptive among you may be thinking, "Ah, he's about to insult Kimihiro Watanuki-kun," or, "This paragraph is going to be mocking Kimihiro Watanuki-kun," but when you realize that, by simple calculations, four out of every 1,461 people in Japan alone must be born on April 1, you will see that this is hardly a problem that affects only Kimihiro Watanuki. It is a matter of the gravest import, beyond all imagining, carved deeply into both Japanese history and educational regulations.

Let me start at the beginning.

A very old joke suggests that people born in a leap year, on February 29, age only once every four years, so that when everyone else born in the same year turns twenty, they are still only five years old. Obviously, this does not actually happen. Why not? Because it has been clearly established that people born on February 29 become a year older on February 28. So what about people born on February 28? They do not age on February 28, but on February 27.

To put things even more plainly, it has been officially declared that leap year or not, every human becomes a year older on the day before their actual birthday. People born on February 29 age on February 28, people born on February 28 age on February 27, and people born on February 27 age on February 26.

As a result of which?

Naturally, people born on March 1 age on February 28 in normal years and February 29 in leap years. Sounds perfectly logical and unremarkable, but this world requires such painstaking logic to allow those born on February 29 to keep their records straight. This allows those born on February 29 to enter the coming of age ceremony with their peers. Congratulations to everyone born on February 29. This nasty little logic puzzle has saved you all.

But where there is light there is shadow. People born on April 1 were left tumbling in that logic's wake. Following the same principles, people born on April 1 age on March 31 . . . but given how the Japanese year is unofficially divided between April and March, that caused all kinds of problems for them. Namely, when it came time for people born on April 1 to enter school, they were forced to enter classes a year earlier than they otherwise would. (Although, legally speaking, they were entering just as they should be.)

Which made them the youngest students in their class . . .

"Watanuki, you're younger than me, and I'm older than you, right? That means I'm superior to you and you'd love to help me out, yes?"

". . . um."

When Kimihiro Watanuki's classmate Sekô Serizawa approached him after class at Cross Private School in a manner that anyone with normal sensibilities would have taken as exceptionally pushy, Watanuki debated for exactly two seconds whether to ignore him and head directly for work, or stay and hear what Serizawa had to say. Quickly deciding that being treated haughtily by his employer was not fundamentally different than being treated haughtily by Serizawa, he chose to listen to Serizawa purely out of a de-

---

* *Coming of age ceremony*   Held annually on the second Monday in January for everyone who will turn twenty (the age of maturity in Japan) during the current school year.

sire to inject some variety into the daily grind, and sat back down in his seat.

Serizawa looked relieved to see that, and sat down facing him, leaning on the back of the chair.

"Sorry."

"Fine."

"Just need some advice."

"From whom?"

"I guess from you, Watanuki."

He guessed?

Okay.

Kimihiro Watanuki did not consider Sekô Serizawa to be anything more than a classmate but neither did he consider him anything less; in other words, they were acquaintances who happened to know each other's birthdays (Sekô Serizawa's was January 13, which Watanuki privately considered to be a small enough age difference to be entirely inconsequential). If they ended up sitting next to each other the next time the seating arrangement changed, and Serizawa happened to forget his textbook, Watanuki would move his desk over so they could share, but that hardly qualified them as particularly close.

At least, that was Watanuki's opinion.

If he defined the distinction a little more clearly and divided everyone into people who knew that Kimihiro Watanuki could see spirits and people who did not, then Sekô Serizawa was one of the people who did not (although it should be made clear that knowing about his sight did not in any way imply that one was close to Watanuki at all . . . like the one with a name suggesting he had a hundred eyes).

---

* *Hundred eyes* Dômeki's name as three kanji: "hundred," "eyes," and "demon."

His eyes.

His sight.

Kimihiro Watanuki's eyes could perceive things that they should not have, that were not part of this world, that should not exist.

His eyes.

He did not feel any particular compulsion to disguise this fact, but neither did he actively go around informing everyone.

"So, what about?"

Of course.

Regardless of what opinions his employer might espouse (that he was prone to violent fits or what-have-you), Watanuki was fundamentally a harmless individual (which, depending on how you look at it, could also be an extremely insulting way of describing him) and whether he was close to the individual in question or not, if someone asked for his advice, he would hardly cut them down. Speaking of cutting people down, Kimihiro Watanuki's favorite member of the Shinsengumi Shogunate killing squad was Serizawa Kamo-sensei, and whatever other objections he might have, a classmate with the Serizawa name coming to him for help was hardly something to be upset by.

"Easy to ask . . ."

"If it's hard to say, should we talk somewhere else?"

"Nah, here is fine."

"Hmm."

Their classroom, after school.

---

* *Serizawa Kamo-sensei*   First leader of the Shinsengumi.

High school students these days were all busy; clubs or sports, cram school, or like Watanuki, off to work. There were only a few people left in the room, and Himawari Kunogi was not among them (this fact was the most critical as far as Watanuki was concerned). If Serizawa said it was fine, there was no reason for Watanuki to insist they go elsewhere.

However.

Despite that, it seemed Serizawa found this very hard to talk about. Watanuki knew any number of people of a dramatic disposition who had a fondness for pausing theatrically before consulting anyone on an issue they had long since made up their minds about, but as far as Watanuki knew, Serizawa's character did not include that particular trait. Did he really put any more stock in age discrepancies than Watanuki did?

Or was— No, Watanuki dismissed the thought before it even formed. That was ridiculous. If that was the case, he could see why it was so hard for Serizawa to speak up—it would be for anyone. But there was no reason for Serizawa to raise a topic like that with Watanuki. Serizawa didn't know about Watanuki's eyes, after all . . .

But Kimihiro Watanuki had forgotten.

It was the founding principle of his life. If there were two possible outcomes, the bad one would always happen to him.

"Right, Watanuki."

"What?"

"I thought I'd talk to you about ghosts."

". . . Oh."

If he had been the kind of person who was able to say that he had just remembered a promise on which his life depended and would have to go home at once, and then just stand up and walk away, Kimihiro Watanuki's existence might well have been more productive, but you could also say that if he had been able to do that, he would not have been Kimihiro Watanuki.

"What a coincidence. I had just been thinking how much I've been wanting to talk with you, to have a good long discussion about ghosts with you."

And with Watanuki's entirely unnecessary protestation of enthusiasm, the conversation continued.

"Watanuki, you ever seen a ghost?"

"Er, um . . ."

Every damn day.

Want to go outside and check if there's some around?

Naturally, he did not say any of this.

"No, I haven't."

Or at least . . .

He didn't want to.

"Yeah, most people haven't. I mean, not like I have or anything. Didn't mean that."

"Oh, really? I just assumed you had. Then . . . Serizawa, what are we talking about? If I've never seen a ghost and you've never seen a ghost, just how are we supposed to talk about them?"

This was hardly the setting for ghost stories.

It was four o'clock, in midsummer, and quite sunny out.

"My kid brother's friend from cram school . . ."

"Mm? Quite a distant connection . . ."

"It gets farther. My brother's cram school friend's club sempai's cousin's college student sister."

"Well, not exactly across the horizon yet. Long as it doesn't get any farther away. Any more distance and we won't be able to see them by virtue of the fact that the world isn't flat after all, but an enormous sphere."

"But college student sister? A college girl."

"That does seem the most likely possibility. Assuming 'sister' is not, in fact, some guy's name."

Fortunately, Watanuki was not the kind of hilarious high school student who begins drooling at the very mention of the words "college girl." What effect those words had on Serizawa remained a mystery.

Either way, Serizawa was asking for advice for his brother's cram school friend's club sempai's cousin's college sister—or, from Watanuki's perspective, his classmate's brother's cram school friend's club sempai's cousin's college sister—who had presumably seen a ghost.

Seeing ghosts.

To Watanuki, that was no big deal, it was a daily/hourly/minutely/secondly occurrence (there was no guarantee that something might not cause him to perceive a horrible spectre over Sekô Serizawa's shoulder at any moment), and that notion alone was hardly likely to surprise him. It probably meant that Serizawa's (omission) college sister had, like Watanuki, a pair of eyes stuffed into her eye sockets which were able to see things that were not there.

Obviously, he had known that he was not the only person able to see spirits. There was, for example, his employer. And it was not at all odd that Serizawa's (omission) college sister was one of them, but this was the first time the subject had ever arisen so unexpectedly, which left a sudden tension gripping Watanuki's heart.

"Mm? What's the matter, Watanuki? You suddenly got all serious."

"Oh . . . no reason," Watanuki said, shaking it off.

The tension had distracted him.

"You're so weird. Why were you giving me the hairy eye-ball?"

"Er . . . didn't mean to." Trying to cover the awkward moment, he forced himself to keep talking. "So, um . . . you can't see ghosts, but this college girl can?"

"Huh? Can't see ghosts? Weird way of putting it, Watanuki—like you're starting with the assumption that ghosts exist. Didn't think you'd be the type to believe in that stuff."

"Oh, I'm not. That was just . . . just a poor choice of words. Said the wrong thing. The point was that it wasn't you we're talking about. But if you're gonna be all picky, I'll rephrase. What you're saying is, this college girl has seen a ghost?"

He recovered quickly, but what he had said was not entirely a lie. Being able to see things was an issue on a different level from actually believing in them. Between the two lay a gulf of terrifying size. If he were able to accept spirits as easily as he saw them, seeing them would not be such a constant source of torment for him. He knew full well accepting them would make things easier for him, but he could not help wishing.

Wishing . . .

. . . that he could not see.

Was Serizawa's (omission) sister the same?

However . . .

"Nah, nah, nothing like that," Serizawa said. "She hasn't *seen* anything."

"This conversation makes no sense."

He was this close to saying something about Serizawa

wasting his time, but he bit it back. If he said something like that he could hardly be upset if word got around that he was prone to violent fits.

"Basically, this college girl . . ."

"Right, this is getting ridiculous. What's her name?"

"Oh, Hôseki Hikage."

"Hôseki Hikage-san? Wow. That's a really bad-ass name. Like something out of a movie."

Without even checking, he was sure Hikage referred to a shady location out of the sun, and that Hôseki referred to beautiful, resplendent minerals. If his employer heard that she would either laugh or scold him fiercely for being so careless, but Watanuki did not consider it all that careless and simply continued the conversation.

"So what about Hikage-san?" he asked.

"Text messages."

"Mm?"

"She keeps getting text messages, on her cell phone."

"From who?"

"From a ghost."

Huh.

How else could he react?

Faced with such a simple statement and such astounding content, Watanuki simply lacked the skills necessary to produce an unexpected and hilarious reaction.

"Let me start at the beginning. Hikage-san had a friend . . ."

"I imagine she did. Most people do. I do, you do, Higake-san presumably does as well."

---

* *Checking the name* Hikage *does indeed mean* "shade"; *and* Hôseki *means* "jewels."

"Yeah, but I meant a specific one. Same major as her in college, name of Kokyû Shikasaka."

"Hôseki and Kokyû? Match made in heaven."

Even more like a movie, Watanuki thought. But there seemed little reason to dwell on that further; it seemed unwise to derail the conversation just as it was beginning to make some kind of sense, and judging from Serizawa's puzzled frown, he was ignorant of any connection between the words "jewel" and "breath," so Watanuki did not pursue it further. At any rate, his classmate's little brother's cram school friend's club sempai's cousin's college sister/Hôseki Hikage's friend, Kokyû Shikasaka-san, had appeared as a new character in Serizawa's story.

"So . . . ?"

"And Shikasaka-san died in an accident last month."

Correction.

Kokyû Shikasaka-san died before she could appear.

"I dunno if it was on TV, but you might have read about it in the papers. I know it jogged a memory for me. Someone died in a station not far from here—college student waiting on a platform got bumped by the train as it came in?"

Watanuki did not remember.

Had he forgotten, or simply never heard about it? He was hardly the type to read the paper wide-eyed from front to back, so it seemed far more likely he had simply missed the story. There were train accidents every day, all across the country, and even if he heard about every single one of them it was impossible to remember them all. Watanuki was forced to admit his ignorance, but Serizawa did not seem terribly put out by it.

---

* *Shikasaka*   The word means "deer hill." *Kokyû* means "breath."

"You know how they always tell you to wait behind the white line? Well, Shikasaka-san was leaning over it a little. She was flung backward, and the back of her head slammed hard into an iron pole that just happened to be behind her. She was in a coma for a while, but never woke up. Cause of death was blunt force trauma and cerebral contusions."

"Trains are like weapons . . ."

"They aren't as bad as cars. But much worse than guns. Not that that's gonna stop me going to driver's school the second I graduate. Anyway, that's all there was to it; not a big deal—I mean, she died, so I guess it was a big deal. Didn't mean it like that."

"I got you. Go on."

"Okay . . . so Shikasaka-san had been planning to get on the train that hit her. She was going to meet Hikage-san. They'd promised to meet in a park somewhere and go shopping together. When she didn't show, Hikage-san thought it was weird, but her friend wasn't exactly a punctual person, apparently, so she just assumed it was the usual and went shopping on her own. She only found out what had happened the next day."

"Must have been a shock."

Just because someone stood you up, you would never dream they had been hit by a train, rushed to the hospital, and died. It was easy to imagine how that felt.

But . . .

That was all there was to it.

Like Serizawa said: No big deal.

There must be more—something bigger.

"And ever since, she gets them."

"She gets what?"

"Text messages," Serizawa said. "Starting shortly after the accident. Every day, every single day, at exactly the time Kokyû Shikasaka was hit by the train, Hôseki Hikage-san gets a message from her . . . even though she's dead."

■ ■ ■ ■

It was my fault.

Kokyû-chan died because of me.

She must have had so many things she wanted to do . . . and it's my fault she never will.

Never—because of me.

If I hadn't asked her to go shopping with me that day . . .

Or if I had gone directly to Kokyû-chan's apartment, instead of arranging to meet elsewhere. I had been to her apartment any number of times, and had a book I needed to give back to her, so it really wouldn't have been all that far out of my way.

And if I'd done that, Kokyû-chan would still be alive.

If I hadn't been so lazy.

If I hadn't skimped on the train ticket for the simple reason that I didn't want to go there and back again. No matter how tight my budget was, I could easily have spared a couple of hundred yen.

Easily.

So she had every right.

―――

Kokyû-chan had every right to hate me.

―――

I had to resign myself to that.

I had to stop resisting and accept that.

It was my fault, you see.

And the most grievous sin was to deny that you had sinned.

But who should I apologize to?

To Kokyû-chan.

But Kokyû-chan was dead.

I was not even allowed to offer an apology.

Or receive forgiveness.

I should not hope for it.

I should not wish for it.

Even if I was given a chance to have any wish granted, I should not wish to be forgiven.

Oh.

When my dear friend Kokyû-chan was dying, what flashed through her mind? As she died, as her consciousness faded away, what drifted across her mind's eye? Or was she in no such poetic state, her mind sinking into blackness without comprehension, without even registering the pain? That would be too horrible. Too horrible for me.

So perhaps she had remembered me.

Perhaps she had known that she would not be able to meet me. Perhaps her final thought, the last thought she would ever think, had been about me.

How silly.

We could have gone shopping anytime.

There was no reason why we had to go shopping that day. Shopping had just been my excuse to spend time with her.

And Kokyû-chan always forgot about little things like agreeing to meet with me. She was always late, she was always standing me up. All the time. I would be pissed at her careless behavior, and she would apologize, and we would be friends again. Like always.

Or was that why?

Because I was always, always, always so angry with her carelessness, always yelling at her for being late . . . so that day she might have been trying to get there on time to surprise me.

She'd been hit at 11:06 A.M.

We were supposed to meet at eleven.

She was already late.

Late like she always was.

That's why . . .

. . . she had been leaning across the line.

In such a hurry, trying not to waste a single second . . .

————

Hurrying to her death.

————

I should have been more patient. I should have been nice to her. Sure, being late all the time was hardly a virtue, but did that mean she deserved to die? Of course not. Nothing about the way she died can be blamed on her.

It was all my fault.

Even my mourning is hypocritical.

I have no more right to mourn than I do to forgiveness. No matter how much I mourn, Kokyû-chan will not come back to life.

I know that.

But if she could, if that were possible . . . I would do anything. I would even trade my life for hers. And I'm not just saying that; that's how important a friend she was.

She was irreplaceable.

And yet . . .

Now that I had lost her, I was sure I would never meet a friend like her, no matter how long I lived. Kokyû-chan was my one and only. I should have treasured her more. It's such a cliché to say that you don't value what is really important, who you really care about until they're gone, but I know it to be true.

Who would ever think?

Nobody would imagine the things and people they care about would suddenly be snatched away from them. It would be like being scared about the sky falling. You couldn't live if you spent your time worrying about something like that.

But I should have.

When I thought about the enormity of what she left unfinished, about what she might have done . . . it hurts so much I feel faint.

What on earth am I to do?

What should I do?

Maybe I should follow her . . .

———

Knnn knnn — my cell phone vibrating.

———

My cell phone — it matched Kokyû-chan's, the same model: au's A5514SA. On the screen . . .

KOKYÛ SHIKASAKA.

The time in the corner of the screen was 11:06 — without fail, the exact time the train hit her.

I opened the message.

My hands shaking as I pushed the button.

---

* *au* One of the three largest service providers in Japan.

I knew it was pointless, I knew there was no meaning, but even as I bit my lip at that knowledge, even as I thought again how much easier this would be if I could just delete the messages without reading them, even though I knew full well it was a crazy thing to do . . . I had to see.

But of course, I knew what it said.

The same message my dead friend sent me every day.

■　■　■

Let us play *shiritori* with shallow dialogue.

Starting with Yûko-san.

" 'P-please! I'll do whatever you say, I'll apologize for everything I've done! I'm so sorry! I beg you, spare my life! I'll pay you two or three times what he will!' . . . L."

To Watanuki.

" 'Liar! An inferior being like you could never hope to match my speed! I'm the best there is! This must be some mistake. Race me again, I'll beat you this time!' . . . M. No, E."

" 'Even so, I would prefer not to. You see, there are some things I simply was not meant to do, and this is absolutely one of them. I must maintain certain *standards*. I'm sure if I put my mind to it I would be perfectly capable, but to do so would simply be beneath me. I've made up my mind! I must be true to myself. That is the long and short of it.' . . . T."

" 'That's what I said! I said it would never work! I knew this would happen. Just as I predicted! I knew it would hap-

---

* *Shiritori*　A Japanese game which requires each player to say a word beginning with the same sound the previous player's word ended with.

pen, I knew it all along. But you didn't listen to me! I warned you! None of this is my fault!' . . . T."

" 'This is what everyone says, so don't go mistaking it for my opinion, but I gotta say, I think you're in trouble. This isn't even about right or wrong, not really. Doesn't matter who's right. I mean, personally I don't have a problem with it, and I'd like to support you, but everyone else? I don't know.' . . . W."

" 'We're done for. We're all gonna die. Damn it! If I'd known this was gonna happen, there was so much I could have done! OOO (heroine's name), I've always . . .' . . . S."

"S . . . sh okay?"

"Fine."

" 'She doesn't understand! Only reason she's still alive is because of me. Because I taught her everything. Without me, she'd be nothing. Just some dumb country girl. So what gives her the right? She doesn't matter to me at all, but she owes me everything! She just doesn't understand.' . . . D."

" 'Don't mean this to sound like an excuse. But I'm sure if you give it some time, and calm down a little, you'll see I did the right thing. No, I don't mind. I'll be the villain this time. I'll take the blame for getting you involved . . . just take it as a small gesture.' . . . E."

" 'Everything in this world has a price! Money is everything! If there was a suitcase full of cash in front of you, you'd forget all about revenge and fall to the ground, swearing fidelity!' . . . Y."

" . . . Yûko-san."

"What? No proper names, you know the rules."

"I know this is putting on airs, but allow me to suggest that this game is not very much fun."

"Oh."

Yûko Ichihara sprawled languidly on the sofa, absolutely immobile, as if she were the sofa's dustcover reborn. For reasons beyond Watanuki's comprehension she was wearing a ten-gallon hat indoors, but you could search the world over and not find anyone dumb enough to mention such a trifling detail to her.

While Watanuki was wearing an apron over his school uniform, with a three-cornered cloth on his head like a cleaning lady (and I need hardly tell you how becoming this outfit was on him), sitting on his knees on a cushion some three paces away from her. To quickly explain, he had just finished basic preparations and had been about to begin cooking dinner when he took Yûko-san a cup of coffee and she had unexpectedly asked him to join her in a game. Once again Watanuki found himself wondering whether the real focus of his duties was the alleviation of Yûko's boredom.

"I find it fascinating."

"I mean, basing a game like this on dialogue means you can manipulate the last letter easily, placing yourself at an advantage."

"And not doing so is a mark of gentlemanly courtesy. Rather like the offside rule in soccer. This is not a game about winning, but about how long we continue, and in what manner we continue. Like two people playing with a bat and a ball. You have to throw the ball where they're likely to hit it. Ending a sentence with X is unthinkable."

"Seems unnecessarily gentlemanly."

"*Shiritori* is a game you should be good at, Watanuki—

---

* *Saving a life*   *Shiritori* saves Watanuki's life in volume 6 of the xxxHOLiC manga.

for your own protection. It may well save your life one day."

"Don't be absurd. You're just trying to pull another fast one on me, but I won't be fooled. There's no way *shiritori* could save your life. If that actually does happen to me some day, I would gladly refund all that I have earned working here so far."

"I will hold you to that."

"Anyway, I don't mind playing *shiritori*, Yûko-san, but at the least we could do 'cool dialogue' instead of 'shallow dialogue.' That would be much more entertaining."

Anything would be better.

Saying that stuff made him feel like he was cutting some unknown but critical part of himself to shreds with a knife held in his own hand.

"The fun comes from reveling in that sensation."

"I hate it."

"But it would never work with 'cool dialogue,' Watanuki," Yûko said. "If we did that, you might think you were *someone*. Give you the delusion that you're the main character."

"Huh . . ."

Strange.

She seemed quite serious suddenly.

"That's a terrible state of mind. The belief that you are the protagonist in your own life is a very dependent way of thought. Downright parasitic. It brings with it the preposterous notion that you're the only one that matters. Even though there are six billion people in the world. And you are only one of them. Even the greatest of them cannot escape that fact."

That's why . . .

. . . it was important to reinforce the fact that you were just a supporting character.

Yûko Ichihara.

The owner of the store where Kimihiro Watanuki worked. The shop where any wish could be granted.

And she was also Kimihiro Watanuki's savior. The savior who would render his eyes unable to see spirits, make them as they always should have been. Of course, this demanded a fair price, which is why Watanuki always came directly here after school, to the shop where wishes were granted, and was forced to dress like a scullery maid and do all kinds of odd jobs. But in return, when he had paid the fair price, he knew that Yûko genuinely had the ability to grant any wish. Otherwise, Watanuki would never have remained in this indentured servitude. Watanuki's values in life were not so unique as to find fulfillment in slaving to the whim of a drunk. They called her the Dimension Witch, but Watanuki knew little about that. He was happy not to—in fact, the less he knew, the better.

Yûko had strange powers, and as long as it was clear her powers would work on his eyes, nothing else mattered. As long as his eyes could no longer see spirits, he wanted nothing else.

So once again today Watanuki had come directly here after school, and was slaving away in his apron . . .

"But that explains it."

Yûko swiveled her neck like a languid snake, apparently tiring of *shiritori,* and gave Watanuki an unpleasantly reptilian smile.

"What happened at school; such a shame. That's why you were a little late today."

Um.

"Yûko-san, I haven't told you about that yet . . ."

It was an old trick, and overused, but awfully easy to fall for when used so blatantly.

"Mm? Oh my, how silly of me. I got the conversation backward again. Very well, Watanuki, I shall allow you to tell me everything you and Serizawa-kun discussed."

"Er . . ."

He was not at all sure he'd ever mentioned that name before . . . but he knew full well that asking would be as pointless as it was sad so he bravely gave up.

"Tell me everything, Watanuki. You see, if this was *Ikkyû-san,* I would be Ikkyû-san."

"If you're Ikkyû-san, then mentioning the name of the show is entirely redundant."

"Then if this were Ankokuji, I would be Ikkyû Sôjun."

"Being more specific just makes it harder to understand . . ."

"And you, Watanuki, are Chin'nen-san."

"Not Shin'emon-san? . . . And I'm really not that familiar with *Ikkyû-san,* but if the kanji *chin* is in the name, then I think it's safe to guess this Chin'nen-san is not exactly the coolest of characters."

"You would rather be Shin'emon-san? I guess you didn't know . . . Shin'emon-san was originally ordered by the Shogun to kill Ikkyû-san. I imagine Chin'nen is looking right for you now, mm?"

---

* *Ikkyû-san* Anime about a child based loosely on Ikkyû Sôjun, a famous Zen monk. Ran from 1975 to 1982 and was highly popular with parents because Ikkyû always outwitted his opponents without resorting to violence. As a boy, Ikkyû Sôjun was placed in a temple called Ankokuji. Chin'nen is a minor character. The kanji for *chin* means "rare, unusual, or strange." Shin'emon is a samurai who becomes friends with Ikkyû. Though a skilled warrior, he ends up hopelessly reliant on Ikkyû to help him out of tight spots.

"Even if Shin'emon-san were as vicious a killer as Okada Izô, I imagine I would still prefer him to Chin'nen-san . . . but it pains me to speak poorly of him without any idea who he is!"

He had never expected his character to be compared to anyone from *Ikkyû-san* in the first place, and nothing in his vague memories of that classic anime allowed him to provide any significant analysis of any similarities to Yûko Ichihara. On the other hand, she did remind him of the real Ikkyû Sôjun, particularly when he began wandering around with a skull on the end of his staff.

"Then forget it. Like before, I am Doraemon."

"That makes me Sewashi-kun . . ."

"From now on you may call me the Fourth-Dimension Witch." Yûko giggled. "Now, continue, Gotanuki."

"No matter how confidently you say that, my name remains unshakably Watanuki, and there's no way you can read the kanji for May first as 'Gotanuki.' "

"Oh? You have gotten uppity, even snide. Like you even know why April first can be read 'Watanuki.' "

"I *do* know that!"

It was his name.

How could he not know?

"You do? You are so learned. Yes, the true reason is that on the first day of the fourth month of the old calender, as one of the traditional events of Shikoku, there was a festival

---

° *Okada Izô*   Samurai from the late Edo period, a feared assassin. Appeared as a character in several movies, including Takashi Miike's *Izô*.

° *Fourth dimension*   Doraemon kept a battery of strange tools in a Fourth Dimensional Pocket.

° *Gotanuki*   Instead of the usual kanji for Watanuki's name (April 1), Yûko used May 1 and made up a likely sounding reading.

where they cut out the bowels of a *tanuki*, and offered them to the gods . . ."

"No! My name has nothing to do with such a grisly rite! Stop it! If you speak in a really deep voice like that, people might actually believe you!"

Obviously . . .

. . . there is not now nor has there ever been such a festival in Shikoku.

Just in case.

"If you don't spill everything quickly, I can keep this up forever. God only knows what I'll come up with for the name Kimihiro. Why is it so much *fun* to make jokes about people's names? The always pleasant sensation of trampling on the rights and dignity of others."

Her eyes glittered like those of a character from an old *shojo* manga. She was behaving quite unnaturally, a little pushy—frankly, a little out of character.

At any rate, it was hardly something he needed to be reluctant to speak about; in point of fact, Watanuki had planned to bring up the topic over dinner. There seemed no point in hiding it any longer, so he told Yûko what Serizawa had told him, almost word for word.

———

Text messages from the dead.

———

Despite bringing the subject to Watanuki's attention, Sekô Serizawa was pretty skeptical about the existence of ghosts, like most people were. But even to someone like Watanuki, who regularly saw spirits, the story was hard to believe. It was also hard to explain, and he kept getting things out of order. He could not get a handle on how Yûko was reacting to it (halfway through she had turned to her side and picked up her pipe, one of the least favorable reactions you could have expected). But at last Watanuki managed to get through everything Serizawa had told him about Hôseki Hikage and Kokyû Shikasaka.

He waited for Yûko to respond.

What part of this disjointed narrative would the owner of the shop where any wish could be granted choose to tackle first? Watanuki was extremely curious to know, and watched her closely, expectantly.

"Interesting," she said, putting her pipe down. "I would never have taken you for a Serizawa Kamo fan."

"And you tackle the least significant part of it!"

"I'm a Sôji fan myself. Just what sort of technique was the Sandanzuki? Striking three places at the same time is physically impossible. Does that mean it was simply a rumor Sôji started himself? Speculating about stuff like that is part of what I like about him. While San'nan was much too cool to be at all interesting. Men absolutely must show off a little."

"I . . . see."

Lots of women liked Okita Sôji, but Yûko's reasons were exceptionally twisted. He had never heard anyone else profess their feelings for Okita Sôji in quite those words.

"If someone has flaws or defects, but that is exactly what draws you to them, people call it *moe*. It's different from 'like,' where you're drawn to their good points, their strengths.

---

* *Okita Sôji* One of the more famous Shinsengumi members and one of their best swordsmen. His most famous sword technique was the Sandanzuki (Three Level Thrust), which could strike the neck and both shoulders, supposedly at the same time.

* *San'nan* Alternate reading of the kanji for Yamanami Keisuke's family name. Second in command of the Shinsengumi, he eventually defected and was ordered to commit *seppuku*.

'Like' doesn't care for defects or flaws. *Moe* is the opposite of 'like' or 'dislike.' So tell me, Watanuki, what about Kamo made you feel all *moe*?"

"No, *moe* has nothing to do with it, I just thought the way Serizawa Kamo lived such a wild life was bad-ass. That's why I liked him. The Mito-han Rôshi, loyalty and patriotism, Serizawa Kamo. I suppose you could say I'm attracted to parts of his personality that I don't have."

"Ha! You lie. You're just showing off, trying to have a better reason than my love for Sôji. Do you really want to impress me that badly? I know full well you're actually a fan of Akane Serizawa."

"What did I ever do to you!? That you would spread such vicious, groundless rumors about me! Akane Serizawa was certainly a good character, but nobody on earth would ever start liking Serizawa Kamo because of her!"

"Personally, I was a fan of Ichijô-san."

"While I can definitely understand that . . . nevertheless! Ichijô-san is certainly a wonderful and universally beloved character, but still!"

But still.

Watanuki quickly forced things back to the original topic, terrified of how Yûko might jack him around if the conversation proceeded to Hibiki Watanuki.

° *Mito-han Rôshi*   A district of Edo-period Japan, part of modern-day Ibaraki Prefecture. *Rôshi* is another word for *rônin*, or masterless samurai.

° *Akane Serizawa*   A character in *Pani Poni Dash* famed for her cat ear hair.

° *Ichijô-san*   Likewise from *Pani Poni Dash* —a mysterious girl who occasionally performs the impossible.

° *Hibiki Watanuki*   A third *Pani Poni Dash* character. Her last name is pronounced the same as Watanuki's but has different kanji.

"That's not the point, Yûko-san. I wanted to know what you thought about the text messages from her dead friend that this college girl, Hikage-san, keeps getting."

"Don't be stupid, Watanuki," Yûko said, calmly, remonstratively. "There's no such thing as ghosts."

Watanuki couldn't speak. Things must be getting a little carried away, because she had just thoughtlessly uttered something she never should have!

"Y-Yûko-san . . . everyone else in the world can say that, but not you!"

"I wasn't joking. Not everything I say is intended for my amusement. Ghosts exist for people who believe in them and do not exist for people who don't. That's the nature of them. Spirits have always been beings that do not exist."

Could he see them because they existed?

Did they exist because he could see them?

Could he see them because they did not exist?

Did they not exist because he could see them?

This was a problem that met all of the conditions necessary for Kimihiro Watanuki to wrestle with it until the end of time, even if his eyes were no longer able to see. And it was exactly what Yûko was driving at.

"What it means is that just as they exist for you, or perhaps in a different fashion . . . Hôseki Hikage can see ghosts."

"Well . . . not see, exactly. She just gets text messages from one."

"Same thing," Yûko said, decisively. "There is no difference at all. If that is what she believes it is, then that is what it is. In a sense . . . she is suffering."

"Suffering? Well, yeah, I suppose she is."

"I did not mean it like that. You know that, Watanuki," she said, without even bothering to check what meaning he had intended. She picked up her pipe again, and put it to her lips, breathing smoke rings around herself—a portrait of ennui. "If it is even that—messages from her dead friend. But from what you've said, they are simply messages sent from her friend's cell phone?"

"Yes, that's right. Like I said, they went out together and bought the newest model . . . I mean, I don't know much about cell phones, but apparently that's what happened."

"Then it seems a logical assumption that the messages are coming not from her dead friend but from a third party using her dead friend's cell phone. A prank, or simple harassment. I would think most people would come up with that theory first."

"Um, well . . ."

Naturally.

When Serizawa told him the story, the idea had occurred to Watanuki as well.

"But the dead friend's . . . Shikasaka-san's cell phone went missing during the accident. They searched the platform and on the tracks, but couldn't find it anywhere."

"Ah," Yûko said. "Missing? Not broken or anything, just missing? That makes it even more likely that someone picked it up and started sending messages. You can't refute the possibility."

"But why? A phone lying on the ground . . . I mean, realistically speaking, someone probably did pick it up and walk away with it, but there's no reason why they would be sending Hikage-san messages like this."

"No, there isn't."

"Or did someone who wants to hurt Hikage-san just happen to pick up Shikasaka-san's phone? That's a huge coincidence . . ."

"There is no such thing as coincidence," Yûko said with a shrug. "Only *hitsuzen*.

"But of course, the flip side of that is that even things that did not occur did not occur because they were not meant to occur—and that is also *hitsuzen*. But perhaps not very realistic."

"Yes. Not very realistic."

"Mm. In which case, we could also say that *hitsuzen* is what led you to think a spirit made the phone disappear."

"Yeah." Yûko seemed to be driving him into a corner, and Watanuki found himself growing more and more defensive. He forced himself to continue.

"And that realistic explanation simply doesn't work, Yûko-san. At least, not with the contents of those messages . . ."

The contents of the messages—the messages that arrived every day at 11:06 A.M. Serizawa had told Watanuki all about them. Watanuki had been reluctant to know the contents of a message to someone else, even if it was from a ghost, even if he had been asked.

". . . this message," he said, leaning sideways to grab a pen and a pad of paper from the staircase chest. He scribbled down the contents as Serizawa had related them.

———

Brave in zero okay?

That -> again eg.

In there only place place frustration eg cell phone eg place in be in okay?

———

"This exact same message comes every time, every day. Never a single letter out of place."

"Hmm," Yûko said listlessly. She stared at the message for a moment, and then passed it back to Watanuki. Before he could say anything, she added, "It's a code."

Exactly.

But it wasn't like any normal code; the sentences weren't even sentences, and if there were really someone sending text messages like this, they were clearly someone not to exchange messages with.

"I see. So this is why she can be so sure the one sending the message is her dead friend. They were the only two people who knew this code."

"Apparently. Their private code. Naturally, Serizawa doesn't know it either. He knew the actual contents, but not what they meant."

Between Serizawa and Hôseki Hikage—Watanuki had already forgotten half of the chain—but there was a brother and a friend and a sempai, and none of them had known how to read it. Only Hôseki Hikage and Kokyû Shikasaka had ever known . . . and now only Hôseki Hikage did.

"Messages in code. Hmm . . . I wonder, is that fun?"

"Probably. Like you have secrets the two of you can share. Not quite a code, but lots of high school girls use smilies and symbols in their messages, so normal people wouldn't understand. Kind of an extreme version of that."

"Ah, well . . . I can understand that, I suppose."

"When Serizawa first told me about it, like you said, I figured it was someone else . . . but if the messages are in a code only the two of them understand . . . I kind of felt a chill run down my spine."

"You did?"

"Well, not literally."

"I see. But Watanuki . . ." Yûko said, pointing with her pipe at the notebook Watanuki was cradling against his chest. "Allow me to point out that that code can be broken."

"Eh?"

"It is not a terribly difficult code. After all, it was created just for fun, and if it was too complicated it would hardly be that. If you really want to create a code that only the two of you can understand, then you can't make it something that anyone could tell was in code; you have to disguise it as an ordinary message. Like that game of *shiritori* a moment before, where the meaning lies in the exchange rather than winning or losing."

"So you can decipher the code?"

"Probably. It's probably Iris."

"Iris?"

"Yes. Of course, I'm just guessing, but odds are I'm right."

Really?

Watanuki thought it looked like the sort of puzzling note someone might make after staying up three days in a row studying for exams . . . but it was just two friends playing around, and a third party with a knack for guessing — someone like Yûko — might well figure it out.

Which meant . . .

"So that means . . . you're convinced this is a prank of some kind? Not a message from the dead at all?"

There's no such thing as ghosts.

Just like she'd said.

"You are a fool, Watanuki. And that particular utterance was the height of your stupidity. Watanuki, the difficulty of the code involved has nothing to do with the situation. What we need to know is if anyone else knew that the two of them had a private code."

"Er . . . um . . ."

Oh. Watanuki nodded.

She was right, the code's complexity was irrelevant. What really mattered was the relationship between Hikage and Shikasaka. If there was a third person involved, then that person would have to have known that the two of them communicated in a private code.

"Right, well . . . just speaking in terms of probabilities, even if only the two of them could read it, it seems likely that people knew that the two of them communicated in code. But in that case, it would be an even more advanced coincidence, since someone who knew that fact would have had to be in the train station when Shikasaka-san died."

"An advanced coincidence? A fascinating phrase," Yûko said, looking quite amused. "Yes, if we're going to suggest something so improbable, than we might as well bring in the idea that this third person murdered Shikasaka-san."

"M-murdered?"

Quite a stunning pronouncement. Watanuki nearly dropped the notebook. Not that it would have mattered if he had, but he found himself hurriedly catching it reflexively. Watanuki's comical reaction appeared to amuse Yûko still further.

"Hardly the sort of notion that should provoke such an obvious reaction, Watanuki. Like you told Serizawa-kun:

Trains are like weapons. And if they are weapons, there are killers who would use them as such. It would be so very simple: Just stand behind them, and give them a little push, and suddenly we have a terrible accident."

"Then . . ."

. . . this was murder?

That was real. This was no time to be talking about ghosts, or messages from the dead.

"B-but according to Serizawa, the police didn't think there was anything suspicious about Shikasaka's death. It was just an accident."

"Oh? Well, even if the accident wasn't an accident, it doesn't explain why this third party—the suspect—is sending her messages from her friend's phone, or why they are using the friend's code to disguise their own identity. The matter is a bit beyond dismissing as a prank or harassment. By the way, Watanuki . . ."

"What?"

"There was one thing you did not explain. Why did Serizawa-kun bring a matter involving the dead to you? Serizawa-kun does not know about your eyes . . . and of course, he does not know about this shop. Which makes it very strange that he came to you with matters of the occult."

". . . . ."

Yûko-san's tone had a ring of conviction to it which suggested she already knew the answer—at least, Watanuki imagined she did. But since she had asked, he could not very well refuse to answer.

"Well . . . 'just because.' "

"Mm? I can't hear you!"

"Fine! Serizawa only talked to me 'because'! And he asked me to pass the story on to other people!"

"Other people?"

"Someone with a name that sounds like they have a hundred eyes."

Yûko Ichihara nodded, clapping her hands.

Deliberately spiteful.

"You mean Dômeki-kun."

"Never mention his name to me again!"

"Right, right, now it makes sense. Dômeki-kun is the heir to a temple almost as important as Ankokuji, and his grandfather . . ."

"Yeah! His grandfather was a pickling stone!"

"I was unaware Dômeki-kun's origins were so very like Son Gokû's."

Shizuka Dômeki.

In a word, Kimihiro Watanuki's mortal enemy. Dômeki could not see spirits, but despite that he could unconsciously drive them away—which was a skill designed to make Watanuki insanely jealous. He did not have what Watanuki did not want, and he did have what Watanuki did want. Apparently he had inherited this skill from his grandfather, a professional exorcist.

"Serizawa seems to have been operating under the mistaken impression that Dômeki and I are friends, which is why he came to talk to me—wanted me to act as go-between, of all ridiculous ideas. I could not be more pissed."

---

* *Pickling stone*   A weight placed on top of pickles to keep them submerged in the liquid. *Tsukemono ishi* is a pun on the grandfather's actual occupation as an exorcist, *Tsukimono-otoshi*.

Essentially, Sekô Serizawa had never expected Kimihiro Watanuki to be of any use at all—he had simply needed an in with Shizuka Dômeki, who was president of a different class. The moment he figured that out, Watanuki found himself tumbling into a bottomless pit of regret, but by then it was far too late.

"Pissed?" Yûko echoed, like she was playing *shiritori* again. "So that's why you told me instead."

"Um, well . . . you did ask."

"But I only did so because you wanted so much to tell me."

Right.

Ignoring her blatant dig for gratitude, he knew perfectly well she was right. He had planned to bring it up after dinner, when she was in a good mood, and that was a fact he could not deny.

He should never have tried to outwit her.

"Yes, given your personality, you could never have taken this story to Dômeki-kun—but that same personality won't let you just forget about this college girl. So you compromised, and brought it to me. I understand."

"But if you put it that way it makes me seem so slipshod and stunted . . ."

"Yes, yes it does. But no matter how you describe it, it could not be farther from your beloved Kamo. Perhaps you should learn a few things from his magnificence, Watanuki. Smooth over your weak spots."

Then Yûko held her arm out toward Watanuki. At first he thought she wanted to shake his hand, but no matter how he looked at it, this was hardly the time for that. After a moment's thought, he realized she wanted the notebook, and handed it over.

"And the pen."

"Sure," he said, holding it out, tip pointed at himself.

Yûko received it, and began quickly writing on the page, though with no signs of interest at all, like a child forcing himself through summer homework, forced to draw the same kanji a hundred times.

"Of course, I shall take a fair price, and add it to your tab like always . . . but what price should Hôseki Hikage pay? Ghostbusting pays very well. Anything connected with death does," she murmured, as if talking to herself.

"I hate to eavesdrop, but I've suddenly been struck with the horrifying thought that the amount of time I'll have to work for you has been steadily increasing all along without my knowledge."

"You must be imagining things."

"Oh, am I? Good."

Yûko handed the notebook back to him.

Below the lines of code Watanuki had written were a few short sentences in Yûko's beautiful handwriting. They were, apparently, the decoded version of the message Hikage received.

As follows:

_____

I cannot forgive you.

Apologize.

You must be punished.

* *I cannot forgive you* . . . This is a translation of the deciphered version of the code. There is no relationship to the coded text in English.

"...................."

"So, Watanuki: You must meet her in the park where she was to meet her friend, at the time she was to meet her friend, and ask her one thing. In addition to the messages, 'Since she died, has Shikasaka-san ever called you?' "

■ ■ ■ ■

She couldn't forgive me.

If she said to apologize I would—if that meant she would forgive me.

If she wanted me punished, I would accept any punishment.

I dream about Kokyû-chan every night.

I think about her awake or asleep, but I know not what purpose it serves. Perhaps it was never meant to have one. Perhaps I simply wish it did. When you get right down to it, human behavior is all impulse and desire.

Whether dead . . .

. . . or alive.

She was my friend, but did I ever really understand Kokyû-chan? I do not even understand myself.

I wonder . . .

What does Kokyû-chan want from me?

What does Kokyû-chan want me to do?

I am not allowed to wish for anything, but what does Kokyû-chan wish for me?

I reached the park.

Eleven A.M.

The park where I was to meet her that day—where I was supposed to meet her and go shopping. It's a promise between Kokyû-chan and me that could never be made again.

In the middle of the park there was a high school boy with glasses, wearing a uniform I often saw in this neighborhood. He was sitting on a bench shaped like an animal overlooking a magnificent fountain. A boy with glasses. No matter how hard I wracked my brain that was the only description of him I could come up with. He was so ordinary if I walked past him on the street I would forget him in a few seconds. He could not produce a positive impression—or even a negative one—not even by mistake. He was a featureless, ordinary, commonplace, and plain boy with glasses. His outline was so indistinct that if life were a TV show he stood no chance of being cast as anything but a hopeless loser and second-stringer. He looked to be so free of personality that he might seriously claim his greatest skill was his ability to perform "Radio Aerobics Two" from memory. Nothing on his person expressed anything about him except his glasses.

And yet, despite all that . . .

Those glasses caught my eye.

No, not the glasses . . .

Those were just a pair of lenses.

Then . . . the eyes behind them.

But even eyes were just a pair of lenses, capable of receiving light . . .

Clutching the phone inside my jacket pocket tightly, as though I were holding Kokyû-chan's hand, I looked around—but there was no one else nearby. Which meant he must be the one who had called. Kimihiro Watanuki-kun. Classmate of a distant acquaintance, Sekô Serizawa-kun . . .

Kimihiro-kun appeared to have noticed me as well. He looked up from his book—no, it was a notebook—and bowed his head at me, without standing up. He did not know what I looked like either, so this gesture was rather nervous and cowardly. I bowed back at once to reassure him. I trotted over toward him, and gave my name, "Hôseki Hikage." I sat on the bench next to the one he was sitting on. Kimihiro-kun was sitting on an elephant, and I was on the giraffe.

"Kimihiro Watanuki," he said. "Sorry about this."

Apologizing already.

Bowing his head seemed to come naturally to him, I thought. Probably spent his whole life apologizing. I had to apologize a lot myself, so I could hardly look down on him for it.

"No, not at all . . . thanks," I said. Having introduced myself, I didn't really know what to say beyond vague formalities. This was a part of me that always use to drive Kokyû-chan up the wall.

But Kimihiro-kun . . . despite having arranged to meet me at eleven, it seemed like he had been here for quite a long time. Less punctual than uptight, I thought. His clothes and mannerisms drove that impression home.

Nothing like Kokyû-chan.

Of course not.

He was much more like me.

Like me.

"Uh, so . . . Hikage-san. Serizawa told me the basic story, but . . ."

"Er, um . . ." There was a long awkward silence, as we both tried to get a read on the other.

Kimihiro-kun had started speaking first, but I managed to stammer a few sounds at the same time. I was always doing this, timing things wrong. Perhaps the most eloquent introduction I could have made. It seemed rude to interrupt him like this, but I couldn't very well stop now, so I continued.

"I don't know what Serizawa-kun told you, but, honestly, I'm fine like this."

". . . like this?"

"Yes."

Kimihiro-kun's reaction was very subtle—nothing obvious, but I could tell the look he gave me was a dubious one.

He thought I was strange.

He thought I was weird.

But that was my honest opinion.

"Kimihiro-kun, your family runs a temple?"

". . . er," Kimihiro-kun said, averting his eyes. "To make it short, something like that, I suppose. According to what Serizawa said, you're getting messages from a friend who has passed away?"

"Yes . . . but I'm fine with that," I said. "Do you think ghosts are a bad thing, Kimihiro-kun? Ghosts, or other . . . occultish things . . ."

"Spirits?" he said, gravely. For some reason.

"Yes, spirits," I said, nodded—the term seemed to fit. "Do you think they're really all that bad?"

"Good or bad, well . . . normally we'd call them bad, right? They hurt people . . ."

". . . and anything that hurts people must be bad?"

The hand in my pocket holding the phone squeezed it tighter.

"Earthquakes are bad? Tsunamis and floods are bad? But those are only happening the way they should, and what happens because of them is what should happen. Even if they hurt people, I don't think they are actually *bad*."

"But . . ." Kimihiro-kun argued, clearly not agreeing. "I understand the logic, but natural phenomena and spirits are not the same."

"Why not?"

"Why not . . . ?"

"I mean . . . she's my friend."

I wasn't saying spirits were good things.

I wasn't saying ghosts were good, either.

But . . .

This was the ghost of someone very important to me.

"Think about it, Kimihiro-kun. If someone important to you—family member, friend, girlfriend, anyone—if someone you cared about died in a tragic accident, would you never hope? Hope that you could see them again, even as a ghost, even as something that wasn't human?"

I was so serious that it silenced Kimihiro-kun.

Had what I was saying got through to him? Or was he just convinced I was insane? I couldn't tell.

I didn't really care which.

Neither one would change anything.

I would never change my mind.

"So . . . do you have to exorcise? I really . . . don't want that. Not anymore . . ."

Tightly, tightly squeezing the phone in my pocket.

Squeezing it with all my might.

"The only thing connecting me to Kokyû-chan is this phone."

I didn't want to lose that.

To lose anything more.

I said so. I had only answered Kimihiro-kun's call, I had only come here to tell him that. I had not wanted to come near this place since Kokyû-chan died. I had not come to the park where I was to meet her to be exorcised . . . I had come to turn down the offer. If he drove her away, it would ruin everything. I dropped my gaze, surreptitiously looking at my watch. 11:02.

Four more minutes.

"I know it sounds strange . . . but I just can't let it go. I can't believe death is the end. Even dead, even as a ghost . . . Kokyû-chan is Kokyû-chan. When we were taking the entrance exams, we were seated near each other, and I borrowed a study guide from her for a last-minute review . . ."

I told Kimihiro-kun how Kokyû-chan and I met. It must have bored him to tears. Nothing less interesting than listening to other people reminisce. But to me, it was a priceless treasure. Each moment of those carefree days was a precious memory.

Memories that were only mine.

They all meant something else now that Kokyû-chan was dead—and I could not accept it.

Could not accept her death.

Even though it was my fault.

Even though I was to blame.

Spirits weren't bad . . .

. . . I was.

"Well, right, I'd agree with that, I guess . . . at least, I can understand it. But Hikage-san . . . the messages you're receiving aren't something you can just ignore."

"I can't? You mean . . . oh, no, didn't Serizawa-kun tell you? They're in code, just a little game Kokyû-chan and I had."

"No, I don't mean that . . . I mean what the code says," Kimihiro-kun said.

I was taken aback . . . for a moment I didn't even grasp his meaning. But it soon became clear he'd broken the code. I didn't think it could be broken that easily, which was why I had told people what the messages said. I guess exorcists were used to this sort of thing? Or at least had a classmate who was a detective . . .

No, wait.

I didn't know if he'd read the message correctly yet.

"Kimihiro-kun, you know how to read the code?"

"Oh, I wasn't the one who figured it out . . ."

I thought not. Kimihiro-kun did not appear capable of anything that impressive. The idea that anyone looks smart if they put glasses on is simply not true. I was sure Kimihiro-kun would be able to write the kanji for the *hekireki* part of *seiten no hekireki* but undoubtedly did not know what *hekireki* meant.

"I know someone whose hobby is being mean and whose job is outright cruelty, and she figured it out. She didn't explain how to read it, just gave me the answer, so I had to think about it for a while . . . but with the answer and the theory in hand, it was like the proofs we have to do in math class.

---

* Seiten no hekireki   A bolt from the blue. The kanji for *hekireki* is rather difficult; it's a word for "thunder" that has passed out of common usage except for this phrase.

But I think I got the answer. Hikage-san, can I see your phone?"

I did as he said, dropping the phone from my left hand into his outstretched palm. I was not a big fan of letting others play with my phone, but I could make an exception.

"Mm, yeah, au's A5514SA. Just like Serizawa said. And Shikasaka-san bought the same one? The phone that went missing after the accident is the same model?"

I nodded.

"Right, that's why Yûko-san was so insistent I make sure they were the same," Kimihiro-kun murmured.

Yûko-san?

Was that the name of his friend whose hobby was being mean and whose job was outright cruelty? I was a little curious what she was like. Really curious, almost eager to find out. How strange.

"So basically, this code is based on the phone's function that suggests words as soon as you start entering them?"

". . . right," I said, nodding again.

He had seen right through me, and hearing those words aloud made me feel like the whole thing had been embarrassingly childish. Having my secret game with Kokyû-chan uncovered was also embarrassing.

"Iris—*Kakitsubata*, right? The basic theory," Kimihiro-kun said. "Predictive text function, a basic feature included in

---

* *Iris/Kakitsubata* The connection between this particular breed of iris and the code may seem a bit obscure, but apparently there is a famous poem from *The Tales of Ise* in which each line begins with one of the five syllables of *kakitsubata*.

* *Predictive text* Predictive text on Japanese phones works in a very different manner than on U.S. phones. Typing one of the 52 kana will bring up a list of common words beginning with that letter. The young women's code involves simply taking that first suggestion every time. It's easy to decipher; all one has to do is take the first sound in each word.

word processing software, specifically designed not for a key-board with more than a hundred keys but for a cell phone, where messages have to be typed using just twelve buttons: zero through nine, star, and pound sign. Each button has five characters, and if you add in alphabet letters nearly ten. Pressing each button over and over to get the character you want takes forever, so cell phone makers have been adding software to get around that for a while now . . . and there are quite a number of different programs out there; au's A5514SA has one of those programs as well. While I doubt you need me to, the simplest way to explain that function is that if you enter あ (*hiragana a*) then it displays a list of words starting with あ at the bottom of the screen. '*Ano*' (that), '*Are*' (that), '*Ai shite iru*' (I love you), or '*Arukikata*' (method of walking). And if you ignored those options, and typed a second character, giving you あ い (*ai*), then the first suggestion would be '*Ai shite iru.*' It would work the same way if you started with か (*ka*)."

Very awkwardly, Kimihiro-kun laboriously explained the code Kokyû-chan and I had used. Ignoring his tone, by this time I'd heard enough to know he was completely correct.

"These programs have the ability to learn, adapting them-selves to the user's needs. Which means words you use a lot are given priority—specifically, if you type い then it will give you the last word you used that started with い. If you typed '*Ano*' just before, '*Ano*' will be first on the list; if you typed '*Are*' then '*Are*' will be first. Which is all foundation stuff. As far as actually reading the code . . . with that infor-mation, it's pretty obvious. You simply create sentences by using the first word the predictive text function suggests. If you want to type '*Kon'nichi wa*' (Hello) you simply type each of those characters—'*ko*,' '*n*,' '*ni*,' '*chi*,' and '*ha*' and select whichever word is first on the list. In most cases this won't generate a sentence that makes any sense. You get a sentence that doesn't even seem like a sentence. If you don't choose the first word on the list but choose likely looking candidates from the list of suggestions you might be able to get something that seems a little more like a sentence, but that would make it less obvious that the message was in code—and with this sort of thing, you need to be able to tell it's in code the moment you lay eyes on it."

With my permission, Kimihiro-kun opened the memo pad on my phone, and typed in "*Kon'nichi wa*"—it came out as "*Konna n de nidai chikyu pasokon.*" (This is two earth computer.) Not exactly a sentence. But I knew what it meant instantly—those were words I'd used on my phone quite recently.

"*Konna*," "*n de*," "*nidai*," "*chikyu*," and "*pasokon*."

"*Ko*" "*n*" "*ni*" "*chi*" "*ha*."

"Voiced and unvoiced consonants turn out the same—this is much less strict than Yûko-san's *shiritori* rules. But with these words already used, the words after this will change . . ." Kimihiro-kun explained.

He must have been referring to how "*ha*" became "*pasokon*." He was right: If you put in "*ha*" "*pa*" "*ha*" in a row like that, they might each turn out as different words. He had more of an eye for detail than I had given him credit for.

"I'm not trying to flatter you, but this is a neat code. Not

---

* *Ha pa ha* Typically consonants in Japanese are unvoiced, but certain characters can be changed to a voiced consonant with the addition of two dots after the kana: は (*ha*) becomes ば (*ba*), for instance. And the *ha* set of characters can also take a small circle, forming a half-voiced consonant- ぱ (*pa*). So why does the "*wa*" from "*Kon'nichi wa*" turn out to be "*pasokon*"? Because that is actually the grammatical particle *wa*—written with the character *ha* but pronounced *wa*.

particularly great as a code, but it works perfectly as a game. If you used a random number table, you'd get a code that no one could break, but this is almost as good. You have to know how the input works on your friend's phone, and the habits it has for suggesting words. The same basic idea, but it doesn't quite work like *kakitsubata*. I mean, if you put in a compound word like '*ningen kankei,*' would you type the whole thing and then change it? Or would you type each word separately? That would change the whole structure of the messages you send in code—it would affect whether typing '*ka*' brings up the word '*kankei*' first or not, and not only that, you'd need to guess correctly how exactly the *hiragana* bits connect to the kanji, making the code even more difficult. And that would apply to more than just the content of the code, right?"

It sounded like he expected an answer from me, so I nodded.

"You can tell from what you just typed in that I had used the words 'earth' and 'computer' recently, right? Of course, this sort of thing only communicates fragments of one's life, but even those tiny scraps of information are a comfort."

A reminder that the sender was alive.

But those . . .

. . . were not my words.

That was what Kokyû-chan had said.

---

* *Ningen kankei*   Human relations.

* *The code*   The Japanese version of the nonsense (coded) phrases translated literally on page 100, as well as the Japanese version of the answer decoded on page 107. Voiced consonants come into play here: *se* becomes *ze*, *ta* becomes *da*, and *sa* becomes *za*. *Wa*, *ha*, and *ba* are covered in an earlier note. And a small *tsu* means the letter that follows is doubled. It doubles the *t* in *tte*, but in the answer it doubles the *s* in *bassarenakereba*.

"Kokyû-chan told me she could tell that I was alive even when she wasn't with me. That's so true. That simple rule saying we had to pick the first word the phone suggested . . . like you said, not only does it make it more like a code, it can mean so much more. I'm sure you've already guessed, but even a simple word like '*Kon'nichi wa*' is seeped in my life — to put it dramatically. Every time I sent Kokyû-chan a message, I was telling her that I was alive."

"If she could parse it," Kimihiro-kun said, curtly, and closed the memo pad. Perhaps he felt a little guilty about this glimpse into my privacy. He quickly opened the notebook he'd been reading when I arrived.

"So you can read the contents of the messages you receive — decipher them. And with a little guesswork, so can other people."

On the page . . . a message in code.

The same message I received every day at 11:06.

————

Yûkiru to wa zero naka ii n desu ka
Ano -> mata rei
Ano naka dake basho basho tte zasetsu rei naka keitai rei
    basho nakarasete naka ii n desu ka

————

"Like I said, it can be a little difficult to decipher unless you know each other really well, but for a passage as short as this, you can get a pretty good idea. Treat it like a proof, and apply a little careful guesswork. The first line breaks up like this: *Yûki/rutowa/zero/naka/iindesuka.* Second line: *Ano/->/mata/rei* — and '->' is what happens when you change '*yajirushi*,' right? So the last line is: *Ano/naka/dake/basho/basho/tte/zasetsu/rei/naka/keitai/ rei/basho/naka/rasete/naka/iindesuka.* Which leaves this . . ."

Kimihiro-kun stopped running his finger along the coded text, and pointed at three lines at the bottom of the page.

The answer.

———

I cannot forgive you.
Apologize.
You must be punished.

———

"But that friend of yours is amazing. I'm not trying to be a flatterer, but . . . Kimihiro-kun, you could figure it out because you knew the answer, right? But your friend did it without any information at all. Without knowing me, without knowing Kokyû-chan . . ."

"Apparently she was able to grab the words that show up repeatedly—'rei,' 'naka,' 'ano,' 'basho,' and 'ii n desu ka'—and extrapolate from there—at least, that's what she says. Despite her efforts to come across like a hermit philosopher, she spends an awful lot of time online. I mean, the phone in the shop is an old black one, but she knew all about cell phones and predictive text functions, which doesn't make sense at all. Is she good with gadgets or not? Going off on a tangent here, but there's something innately ominous about those old black phones. Not that I'm particularly cell phone savvy, what with school regulations. She's definitely good with weirdness. She's the kind of person who bases her entire life on accessing the Akashic Records."

Her hobby was being mean, her work was outright cru-

° "Gadgets" and "weirdness" are homonyms in Japanese; both read as *kikai*.

° *Akashic Records*   All world knowledge, recorded in a mystical plane of existence.

elty, and her entire life was based on accessing the Akashic Records? Certainly a most curious individual, but also one I absolutely did not want to meet.

Well.

Not that there was much chance of that.

I was absolutely sure that would never come to pass.

I would never meet her.

I glanced at my watch.

11:05.

One more minute . . . a few dozen seconds.

"This isn't a cheap mystery novel, and me going on explaining all this is a little bit pointless . . . but if everything I said was accurate, then . . . Hikage-san. If there are good and bad spirits, then this one is clearly bad."

"Why?"

"Wh-why? But . . ."

"But it's my fault."

The words I'd been telling myself over and over all month long, and now I said them aloud so Kimihiro-kun could hear. They were carved into my mind, like stage directions, like fine print.

Words of self-blame.

Words of self-abuse.

"It was my fault. My fault Kokyû-chan died. I killed my friend. So it's only natural. Kokyû-chan has every right to hate me. 'I cannot forgive you. Apologize. You must be punished.' She's right."

———

"I must be punished."

———

"But . . . Shikasaka-san was . . . It was a sudden train accident, right? There wasn't anything suspicious about it. Hikage-san, you aren't . . ."

". . . Legally responsible? No. But that doesn't matter. She was my friend! She was my friend, and that accident would never have happened if it weren't for me. If I hadn't yelled at her all the time about being punctual . . . she might still be alive. Or if I had gone to her house to meet her . . ."

"Hikage-san," Kimihiro-kun said, his eyes looking very sad.

Those eyes, through his glasses.

Was that sympathy?

Sympathy for who? Me?

Then sorry, but please stop. Nothing I just said deserves any sympathy at all. I absolutely do not want it. Seriously, I'm not allowed to accept your sympathy. People repenting must not ask God for salvation. I had not yet lowered myself to do anything so detestably calculated.

It's not for me.

Keep your sympathy for Kokyû-chan.

She had a friend like me, and because of that she lost her life. Poor, poor Kokyû-chan . . .

"Kimihiro-kun . . . this is the way things should be. If Kokyû-chan has . . . is a ghost, a spirit, even if she is trying to harm me . . . even if Kokyû-chan is an evil spirit . . . then that's the way things are. Even if all that is true, I forgive her. I believe she has every right to hate me . . . even if Kokyû-chan kills me, I have no complaints."

"Even if she kills you?"

"Perhaps I should be dead."

If only . . .

. . . I had the courage to die. But I could not follow her. I was too afraid. And that was my great shame . . .

11:06.

Within this minute, that message would arrive, received by the phone in Kimihiro-kun's hands. The longest sixty seconds in my day.

"So. I'm very grateful to you for being nice enough to call me here. But . . . sorry. I don't need to be exorcised. I'm fine with this. I have no problems with my current situation. The messages she sends to my phone prove that Kokyû-chan is still connected to me. They tell me she is still alive . . ."

"Um . . ." Kimihiro-kun said, at a loss for words. Now I knew for sure: It was not sympathy in those eyes, but shock. He must have been absolutely disgusted with me.

I didn't care.

In my pocket, I tightened my hand.

And . . .

———

Knnn knnn—my cell phone vibrating.

———

Artificial lights flashed on my phone, in Kimihiro-kun's hand. The display read 1 NEW MESSAGE. And Kokyû Shikasaka's name . . .

"Um, Hikage-san . . ."

But . . .

Kimihiro-kun ignored it completely. He turned to me and asked . . .

"In addition to the messages . . . since Shikasaka-san died, has she ever called you?"

The moment he said that . . .

I dropped the phone from my pocket.

■ ■ ■ ■

When Kimihiro Watanuki returned from the park with a fountain to the nameless shop Yûko Ichihara ran, where any wish could be granted, she was sprawled like a dustcover on the sofa in her ten-gallon hat, just like the day before. But while she had been lying facedown yesterday, today she was on her back—a dramatic change that quite astonished Watanuki.

No.

He was not so easily astonished.

But he did feel a need to ask the reason.

"Mm? Well, you see, Watanuki, if you lie in the same position for too long you will eventually get a bedsore. This simply proves how much attention I pay to my looks and health."

"No, not the reason you turned over."

Not any such ordinary reason.

Watanuki placed on the table the notebook he had taken with him to the park, and placed next to it the phone Hôseki Hikage had dropped from her pocket an hour before, at 11:06.

Yûko glanced sideways at the phone.

"No doubt about it?"

"Hunh? What do you mean?"

"Of the two phones, this one did not belong to her? The same type, the same model, so are you sure this is the one? You can be awfully careless, and frequently make sad mistakes like that. Just to be sure."

"Yeah . . . well . . . they're even the same color."

It was only natural for someone who had not been there to think they might have been switched. But as Yûko had suggested, he had been holding the phone, on the flimsy excuse that he needed it to explain the code. The difference had been clear. Even while he had been carrying out Yûko's instructions Watanuki had had no idea what he was trying to accomplish . . . but no matter how careless he may or may not have been, it was impossible for him to have made a mistake.

"But as far as which was hers . . . they both were, right? She had both of them, after all."

"No," Yûko said, shaking her head.

Both positions seemed equally arrogant, but Watanuki was quickly discovering that speaking with someone lying on her back required more than three times the self-control demanded by normal conversations. When animals showed their bellies they were being submissive, but with people it appeared to be the height of scornful contempt. Perhaps it required less self-control than forbearance.

He could smell booze.

She had quickly hidden the bottle when she heard him coming, but apparently she had been drinking all morning. She seemed less like the Dimension Witch who could grant any wish and more like the drunken master. None could surpass her if she only had her liquor! Watanuki silently vowed never to be like her, even if it meant his wish was never granted. She led by anti-example.

And given how much she indulged her vices, Watanuki was at a loss to explain how she had functioned before he started working for her.

If I were ever to quit, she would die of malnutrition or alcohol poisoning within a week . . . I am Yûko-san's lifeline.

This thought allowed him, barely, to forgive her haughty manner and insulting posture.

At ease once more, Watanuki asked, "No? No what?"

"This is Kokyû Shikasaka's phone, Watanuki."

That stopped him.

"Unshakably and absolutely. At least, as far as Hôseki Hikage is concerned. Yes. Exactly. This means she has paid her fair price. Prosperity and comfort to us both."

". . . I'm totally lost."

"That is because you are an imbecile."

"Oh? After all the work I've done for you?"

The moment he had asked what Yûko had instructed him to ask—"Has Shikasaka-san called you?"—Hôseki Hikage went white as a sheet, visibly shaken. She jumped to her feet, not even attempting to pick up the phone that had fallen out of her pocket. Instead she grabbed her phone out of Watanuki's hands and ran out of the park. Watanuki was left sitting alone and baffled—and eventually he had given up and come back here, without understanding any of it. He had worked out the explanation of the code on his own, but that hadn't required a great deal of brain power; Yûko had already done the bulk of the work for him.

He had to know more.

"You've got a lot of nerve asking me to explain from one to ten, Watanuki. You should try to think for yourself sometimes."

"I'm far too worried about surcharges to ask you to explain all the way up to ten, but could you at least tell me what one is? Then I might be able to prove that I'm a clever boy and able to guess ten from one."

"Hmmm . . . I've never seen you so intent. Not like you at all. Most vexexing."

"Did you just stutter?"

"No. Merely a typo."

"Only you could mess up admitting you messed up."

Yûko slowly sat up— No, she started to, but then got too lazy and sank back into the sofa like a child who can't do sit-ups.

Languidly.

But her eyes, as they stared up at the ceiling, were captivating.

They clashed fiercely with her posture.

"It's really not that difficult. You saw everything that was happening with your own two eyes. The ghost was really zebra grass—nothing else to it. The messages from her dead friend were sent by her to her own phone every day at 11:06. A tragic little farce, written by and starring herself," Yûko said, looking ever so bored.

"Yeah, well. I did actually figure that much out . . ."

He wasn't *that* stupid.

What he couldn't understand was why she'd had two phones. The one she let Watanuki hold, and the one she'd been gripping tightly in her pocket—the one that was now lying on the table in front of him.

---

* *The ghost was really zebra grass*   *Yûrei no shôtai mitari kareobana* appears to be a Japanese saying that means, essentially, that what appears to be supernatural and frightening is actually something very ordinary.

When Watanuki had typed "*ni*" as the first word, the predictive text had produced the word *niðai,* or "two."

"In other words, like today, she used the phone in her pocket to send a message she had typed out in advance to the phone I was holding. That much I understand. She was looking at her watch an awful lot. But isn't that . . . weird?"

"Weird? Why? Certainly, it is quite odd," Yûko said, as if rebuking Watanuki for his lack of comprehension . . . but with a touch of mischief. "You have to admit, it fits the facts. Not one inexplicable thing happened. Before we think about other people and suspects, before we assume the messages came from a ghost, we should be, well . . . realistic. She knew the code. Undoubtedly. So there was no need for advanced coincidence. All we needed . . . was *hitsuzen.*"

"I don't get it. You mean, that . . ." Watanuki said, pointing at the phone on the table. "That phone is the one that was lost during the accident? Kokyû Shikasaka-san's phone, that Hikage-san somehow found . . . ?"

"Hardly. That is such a simple way of thinking, Watanuki. She was waiting in the park; how would she have found the phone her friend lost in the station? The real phone was probably picked up by some stranger, or just kicked away somewhere."

Simply lost.

Like phones were every day.

"That's so . . . normal."

° *Niðai*   The first character in this word means "two," but the second word is a counter. Many different counters—words that combine with the number-kanji—are used in Japanese to describe how many of something there are. Cell phones happen to be counted with -*ðai.*

"Losing things, losing important things, people you care about dying . . . that's just normal, isn't it? Absurd, isn't it, that some people simply cannot understand that. Once something is lost . . . it is too late."

Watanuki waited.

"So this phone is a replacement, Watanuki. That is why it has value as a fair price. Shikasaka-san died last month? After that, Hikage-san bought a new phone, with a new contract."

"A new . . . contract?"

"In this instance the word has no deeper meaning than the agreement she signed with the cell phone provider. But, Watanuki. When Serizawa-kun told you this story, did you not notice anything strange? I mean, Shikasaka-san was dead. Whether her phone was lost or not, her contract with the provider was over. That sort of thing costs money, you know. Her family would have canceled it. When the phone vanished or was simply lost, it doesn't matter. When you get right down to it . . . cell phones are just machines."

If you die . . . the contract ends.

Canceled . . . or broken.

Of course, Watanuki thought. It was so obvious he had never noticed. Cell phones were hardly magic, but a perfectly ordinary, contract-based societal system.

Which meant . . . for a few days after the accident, maybe, but a whole month later? Nobody would be able to use that phone. And Kokyû Shikasaka only began sending messages to Hôseki Hikage's phone a few days after the accident.

A sinister discrepancy.

Downright backward.

"What does it mean, Yûko-san?"

"Nothing justifying that grim tone. You should have said brightly, 'Say what, Yûko-tan?' subtly playing up the intimate bonds between us while showing off your mental strength."

"Even in my next life I will not need that kind of mental strength."

"You just don't get it."

"In all the time I have served you, Yûko-san, I have never once known the sublime pleasure of understanding a thing you have said."

"Oh. Then let me put it simply," Yûko said, kindly.

A particularly phony sort of kindly.

"It's very simple, Watanuki — Shikasaka-san's family canceled her cell phone contract, and Hikage-san bought a new phone — obviously, the same kind as Shikasaka-san had used before, the same kind she herself owned, since the whole thing was meaningless otherwise. Owning several different phones is hardly unusual these days. And as soon as she signed the contract, she set up the text messaging address."

"Oh!" Watanuki yelped, and immediately clapped both hands over his mouth.

Yûko's grin, stretching from ear to ear, was one of immense satisfaction.

"Such a transparent response. Thank you. Yes, you get to decide your own address for text messaging — and naturally, Hikage-san selected the one Shikasaka-san had used before her death. They were friends, so she had that address in her address book. The address had been used until right before she claimed it, so her chances of getting it were very high.

And the kind of person who would exchange messages in code is unlikely to choose an address in high demand. Once she had the address, the phone was ready, and she could begin. She sent herself messages from that address to her own phone . . . every day at 11:06 A.M. The messages arrived at her phone from Shikasaka-san's address, just as her address book said. At least, that was what the screen displayed. The same company, the same domain, everything exactly the same."

"So . . . that explains the bit about the ghost calling her?" Watanuki asked, remembering how Hôseki Hikage had reacted when he asked that question.

She had been able to choose the address freely, but phone numbers were not as easy to obtain. It was virtually impossible for Hôseki Hikage to acquire the number Kokyû Shikasaka had used. Which meant Kokyû Shikasaka would never call her.

And so . . .

. . . she had run away.

Leaving the phone as a fair price.

"More of a con than a trick," Watanuki said.

"That may well be true. If you take that whole drama as an attempt to con herself. But by the same logic, the trick with the cell phone contract and the mail address could have been duplicated by anyone, and in and of itself does not prove that she was the one behind it all. But since the message was in code, that meant it was either a ghost, or her. And she seemed much more likely."

"Because there's no such thing as ghosts?"

"Exactly," Yûko said, using the armrest on the couch to

stretch her neck. Her haughty manner grew even more arrogant. The ten-gallon hat fell off, dangling from her narrow
neck by the string tied beneath her chin. "That's why she had
to *create* one."

"Create?"

"She created Kokyû Shikasaka's ghost. That is why the sec-
ond phone was not Hôseki Hikage's, but Kokyû Shikasaka's.
Watanuki, if you want to make a ghost, you can. Anybody can.
I could easily make a *god*."

Made a ghost.

Made one up.

Created a spirit.

*"Think about it, Kimihiro-kun. If someone important to you —
family member, friend, girlfriend, anyone — if someone you cared
about died in a tragic accident, would you never hope? Hope that you
could see them again, even as a ghost, even as something that wasn't
human?"*

Hôseki Hikage's own words. So earnest, so sincere. Had
she meant them like this? Then that explained why she did
not want to be exorcised. Nobody wanted to see something
they had created be destroyed.

But that meant . . .

"In that case, why did Serizawa bring this to me? Or not
to me, but to a certain pickling stone heir I do not wish to
name aloud? If it was all just a performance, and all for her
own benefit . . . why wasn't she satisfied with that?"

"That is how amateurs think, Watanuki. You must stop
blurting out everything that pops into your mind. Watanuki,
what do you think spirits *need*? What do you think makes
them what they are?"

"Need?"

He had never even wondered.

To Watanuki, spirits were just something he could see, just something that was always there, something so commonplace he couldn't even begin to imagine what spirits might need to make them spirits. It was just like asking what made humans human . . . No.

No, not "just like."

The same.

"They need to be perceived, Watanuki. That is why people like you, who can see spirits, are so important. You can perceive spirits despite all logic and science. And that is valuable, both to humans and to spirits."

There was even a technical word for the ability, Yûko explained: *kenki.*

This bit of trivia dispensed with, she continued,

"But with someone who does not have your ability . . . if you want them to be aware of spirits, what can you do? The simplest method is to make them believe."

"Make them believe . . . that something is there? That *is* a con."

"Absolutely."

"But in this case, it was an awful lot like a con, but there wasn't actually a ghost."

"Like I said, there is if people think there is, and there isn't for people who think there isn't. A being that does not exist. But in this case, Hikage-san knew the truth. She knew that Shikasaka-san had not become a ghost—after all,

* *Kenki* The first kanji is "see," the second is "demon."

she had made the whole thing up. And you can't lie to your-self."

"And that means the ghost doesn't become real?"

"That's why she had to make everyone *else* believe."

Make them believe . . .

. . . so that the ghost could take form.

There are a great many strange things in the world, but no matter how odd, how incredible something may be, if a human does not touch it, if a human does not see it, if a human is not involved with it . . . it is simply a phenomenon.

Simply a matter that will fade with time.

"Even if you can't lie to yourself, you can lie to other peo-ple. Why did Serizawa-kun bring the story to you? That's be-cause Hikage-san needed him to. Serizawa-kun's brother's cram school friend's club sempai's cousin's college sister was Hikage-san, which shows you just how many people had be-come aware of Shikasaka-san's 'ghost.' So many people you had to start skipping people on the chain when you said it aloud. All of them knew the story. And since it was basically a pyramid scheme, the number of people who knew was even larger."

"So . . . basically, strength in numbers? The more people knew about the ghost and believed in it, then even if she knew it was a lie . . ."

Kokyû Shikasaka, her irreplaceable friend, would still exist. Exist without existing, but exist nonetheless.

Serizawa had been dismissive.

But he had not dismissed it.

Otherwise, he would not have come to Watanuki, trying to get word to an exorcist's grandson like Dômeki.

"By this point, even she was aware of Shikasaka-san's ghost. Like I said. A con. She conned herself. Spirits that are not perceived might as well not exist . . . so a spirit that many people are aware of? Even if it does not exist, that is the same as if it does. That is how you make a ghost. You see, Watanuki? Hikage-san needed to tell everyone her dead friend was sending her messages. To make the ghost into a ghost, to make the spirit into a spirit."

Needed.

Then Watanuki himself . . . had just been fulfilling that role. He had been absolutely aware of Kokyû Shikasaka's existence, and the messages she was sending.

His eyes.

Even without them, there were things that could be perceived.

"Rather pathetic of me . . . but the whole story is pretty sad. Her feelings for her friend were so strong, so very strong that she made her into a ghost. Caring about friends is a good thing, but I could never do something like that."

Had he ever felt that keenly about anyone? He had good friends, and he had a family. He had a girl he liked. But were his feelings for them so powerful that he would make them into ghosts if they died?

He might have eyes that could see spirits.

But that did not mean they could see who was important to him.

"You have seldom been more foolish, Watanuki. You make it sound like this is a *good* thing."

Yûko's excessively snide comment interrupted his thoughts. There was a mocking smile on her lips, a sneer.

"Er . . . isn't . . . it?"

"Hell no. Watanuki, you really are a sucker. You think I'd be involved in anything good? This is a terrible affair, an ugly story. Someone who makes their precious friend into a spirit does not care about their friend. Quite the opposite, Watanuki. Hikage-san is, in my opinion, incredibly selfish, and horribly egotistical."

Watanuki simply could not understand what she was saying. The girl he had met in the park, the story she had told him . . . bore no resemblance to Yûko's words. After all . . .

"After all, she only thought about herself," Yûko said. "Didn't you notice, Watanuki? She was talking about her feelings all the time. Obsessed with herself. Disgustingly self-centered."

"But that . . ."

" 'I must be punished'? What mattered to her was not the 'must be punished.' Just the 'I.' "

———

"And no dialogue could be more shallow than that."

———

Something in her tone caused Watanuki to choke back his words.

But, now that she mentioned it . . . it was true. When he had been talking with her, Hôseki Hikage had said the word *watashi* rather a lot. Far more "I" than "Kokyû-chan." Japanese grammar frequently omits the first-person pronoun; but this woman almost never did.

° *"I"*   One of the unique features of the Japanese language is that subjects can be left out if they are understood. Most people tend to avoid using first-person pronouns excessively for fear of sounding self-absorbed.

But if Yûko hadn't pointed it out?

She had not even been there, so how had she been able to hit the nail on the head like that? This could not be dismissed as a good guess. Watanuki took a step backward, as if in fear. Yûko's smile broadened still further.

"Always look out for people who use too many first person pronouns. Hikage-san talked about herself the whole time she was with you, right? I, I, I, I, I. From what she said, did you get any sense of what Shikasaka-san was like?"

"Er . . . well . . ."

"Of course you didn't. You can't even begin to imagine Shikasaka-san's personality or character, can you? You don't even know what she looked like, how she dressed or wore her hair. You could never draw a picture of her from what Hikage-san told you. You could sift through the whole thing and only come up with a single trait—the lack of punctuality that may have brought about the accident. But even that was little more than an excuse to prove that she herself *was* punctual. It is interesting how punctual people always have friends who are never on time. All people look for qualities they lack in others. Character traits, abilities, status, money. *The Prince and the Pauper.* Or, for that matter, Jewels and Breath. Ah ha ha. That one might be going too far. When you get down to it, love is the same, genders are the same. The difference between like and *moe*, how *moe* contrasts with love and hate. Love and hate are both emotions for yourself. Opposites do attract. To complete yourself, you need others. The same way a weakling like you idolizes a wild nutbar like Serizawa Kamo, she looked for what she lacked in Shikasaka-san. She saw other people only as a mirror for herself."

"B-but . . . Yûko-san. It was all blaming herself, abusing herself. Hikage-san felt responsible for Shikasaka-san's death . . ."

"Do you really think that?" Yûko said. "If your friend was running late, leaned over the white line, and was hit by a train and died? Who would you blame?

"No matter how you look at it, only Shikasaka-san bears any responsibility for her death. It was her stupid mistake, her fatal error. Inarguably her fault. Only Shikasaka-san had anything to do with Shikasaka-san's death. Nobody else can barge in there. Grieving is one thing, but there is nothing for Hikage-san to regret. Quite the opposite. But she used her friend's death so she could play the role of the tragic heroine. She was the same with everyone. It was all just a perfor- mance."

"But isn't that a twisted way of looking at things? A mali- cious interpretation? According to what she said, Hikage-san was always arguing with her about how late she was, and that was why she was in such a hurry that she let herself get hit by the train . . ."

"You're thinking too much." Yûko shook her head dis- missively. "I may have said 'no matter how you look at it' — but looking at it from that point of view is obviously abnormal. And with humans, being careless with time is not a personality trait, but something innate. Something they will never correct. If they really wanted to, they'd need profes- sional help . . . conflict with a friend would not even rattle them. Shikasaka-san was late like always, and just happened to step across the line. It stands to reason that the accident was her fault. It was her fault she was late, her fault she stepped over the line, and has nothing to do with anyone else. Hikage-san's interpretation can only be explained as forcibly involving herself in her friend's death. Calling attention to herself."

"Then . . ."

"Self-centered people prefer to control everything, to organize everything so that they are in charge, to try and claim all the credit, and to give up completely if their opinion does not win out. Everyone knows this. But that is not all, Watanuki. Quite a lot of people who seem to be quite the opposite—people who think everyone is out to get them, people who think they are causing problems for everyone else, people who doubt themselves, people who deny themselves, people who sacrifice themselves, people who abuse themselves, people who blame themselves—all of these people are also extremely self-centered."

"They only ever think about themselves . . . ?"

I.

Me.

Myself.

Feeling responsible for everything—believing it is all your fault.

How arrogant was that? How self-important?

Taking blame that rightfully belonged to others, burdened by guilt that should be carried by others, stealing other people's work.

Her friend had died, but that didn't change anything. She never mourned at all, just wondered what she could have done, thought about what she had failed to do—repented, regretted, and thought only of herself.

And eventually made up a ghost.

My precious friend.

The ghost of a friend . . . who was very dear *to her.*

A tragic farce written by and starring herself—and only herself.

"The mistaken belief that you are the protagonist—the delusion that you're the only one that matters. Even though you are only one of them, as is every individual, as is every human. Four out of every 1,461 Watanukis are born on April first, and one out of every 1,461 people are born on February twenty-ninth. But there are six billion people on the earth. Some are better off than others, but they are all people. It is only natural for the most sad and insignificant person to believe that they are special, but you must never imagine you are the main character. I know it sounds like a heavy-handed moral, but there it is. If you really care for your friends . . . you won't turn them into spirits. You will pray for their safe passage. No matter how much you want to see them again . . . you should not meet with someone dead."

At last, Yûko sat up.

This time successfully.

She picked up the phone.

"This is the shop where wishes are granted. People who can grant their own wishes cannot come in, cannot even see it. I will never meet Hikage-san. In that sense, there really was no reason for Hikage-san to pay a fair price . . . but since I did do some work, I have no choice. That too . . . is *hitsuzen.* We could also call it payment for successfully spreading knowledge of the ghost . . . Hikage-san never guessed it might reach the ears of the real thing—like you, Watanuki. Or Dômeki-kun—he might have saved her too, but not in the same way. And this might well have been what she really wanted—to take responsibility for what she had done. Was I being a pushy salesman again this time, Watanuki?"

"Not wanting to become a pressed flower, I said nothing."

"Oh? Very wise. You have at last achieved the right frame of mind to work here. Splendid. Now, to work!" Yûko exclaimed brightly. She opened the newly acquired cell phone, stabbing it with her thumb.

"Oh expressionless skull, so free of hate, how grateful I am to you. There is nothing more I can say . . . *Kyôunshi.* Be well, be well."

It appeared Yûko was busy typing a text message. While she did not look at all accustomed to using cell phones, she was tapping out the message at impressive speed.

". . . What are you doing?"

"Mm? Send, ing, a, message, to, a, friend. I may not, seem it but I am . . . quite fond . . . of writing letters."

As she finished answering, she finished the message, and snapped the phone shut. And as if it no longer mattered to her at all she tossed the phone over her shoulder, turned toward Watanuki, and flicked on a bashful smile, as if changing the channel, and said, "Watanuki, what kind of *shiritori* shall we play today?"

■ ■ ■ ■

No.
No no no no no no no no no no.

° Kyôunshi   Another name for Ikkyû. This is one of his poems.

It wasn't me, it wasn't me, it wasn't me, it wasn't me, it wasn't me, it wasn't me, it wasn't me, it wasn't me.

Kokyû-chan was sending those messages.

Kokyû-chan was sending those messages to me.

Kokyû-chan was alive.

Alive inside of me.

I wasn't lying.

It was my fault Kokyû-chan had died, it was like I'd killed her, so I had to do everything for her, I had to take any judgment, any punishment, I could not be forgiven, I had to apologize, I had to think, I had to wonder what I could have done if I'd been there, I had to calm down, if I were calm, I might have been able to guess what was happening but I was so distracted, I had to be careful, I had to be more cautious, what could I do for Kokyû-chan, I was so bad at this but Kokyû-chan was my friend so I had to think of her and do my best but I'd been so sloppy, I was so proud of Kokyû-chan, I just had to brag about her but I just wanted to help, I just wanted to do anything for her, I didn't really matter, Kokyû-chan was more important than me, I had to put her before myself, it was my fault, all my fault, did I even matter to Kokyû-chan what did Kokyû-chan think of me, me, me, me, me, me, me, me, me, me, me, me, me, me, me, me, me, me, me!

———

Knnn knnn—my cell phone vibrating.

———

It caught me by surprise. I shivered.

I opened the phone. New message.

Addressed, of course, to me.

From, of course, my dead friend.

Even though it wasn't 11:06.

I had done nothing.

I took my right hand out of my pocket.

See?

My friend was alive.

Alive because of me.

Me.

Me.

———

PM message so

Hotel purchased so basically thing only earth basically that book
    purchased next month

Oh only PM so where

———

"Huh?"

———

Sorry.

Plans with other friends . . .

. . . see you some other time.

———

Which is why I call this the Eye World theory.

But I imagine this childishly simple bit of logic will not be enough to convince you. Logic must always be accompanied by more responsible facts. This is something I have insisted upon my entire life. To prove my own accuracy, my own correctness, beyond a shadow of a doubt, I cannot offer myself as the only example. In light of which I would like to introduce a certain boy to you, a perfectly ordinary, commonplace example.

His name is ■■■■■■■.

A ■ year high school student at ■■ Private School, he is ■■ cm tall, and weighs ■■.■ kg—a slender, frail-looking boy. He is very good-natured, not at all shy, but I'm afraid he does have a tendency to get worked up about things. In other words, a perfectly ordinary adolescent. He was born ■■, ■■, his sign is ■■, his blood type is ■, and his family are ■■■■■■■■■■■■— rather a complicated situation. ■■■■,■■■■■■■■■■■■■■■■. His vision is ■/■. ■■■■■■■■■. Which means he has every qualification and quality needed to be part of my research data. ■■■■■■■■.

Yes.

He can see.

Things that are not human.

Things that are not part of this world.

Like my own, his eyes have capabilities well beyond the understanding of modern science, problems that must be addressed by the next generation of scientists. Any number of things I have proposed in this theory have already been largely dismissed. But as a counterexample, the ■■■■ theory is based upon the ■■ ■■■ techniques proposed in the 17th century, but they apply specifically to this boy. ■■■■■■■■, ■■■■.

That would be spirits.

Spirits.

Things that are always around us, but which we cannot normally perceive.

Things we should not see.

Things we should not be able to see.

████, ██████████, ██████████.

He would like to stop seeing them.

Since I too was a ████, I expected great things from his eyes that could see things that did not exist. But the world they perceived was far beyond my imagining. The existence of ████ not only supported my Eye World theory, it completely confirmed it.

I now had the foundations.

████, ████████████████████████████, ██████████

██████████, ████████, ██████████████████. Because of that, he is enduring hard labor at a certain shop. Profitless, pointless, fruitless, meaningless, and unrewarded work. He was an excellent subject, but psychologically unsound. Even allowing for his age, ████████'s mental frailty was obvious. This proved that his ability was acquired, not congenital. As for the shop in question, it was ██████████. Located in ██████████, but not everyone can enter it. ████████, ██████. Only those with a strong desire can enter.

That shop grants those desires.

The shop's owner is named ████████, but that has little to do with my theory.

■ ■ ■ ■

There are a great many strange things in the world.

———

But no matter how odd . . .

How incredible something may be . . .

If a human does not touch it . . .
If a human does not see it . . .
If a human is not involved with it . . .

It is simply a phenomenon.
Simply a matter that will fade with time.

Humans.
Mankind.
Homo sapiens.

Humans are the most profoundly mysterious living things in the world!

■   ■   ■

"I found this wallet."

Kimihiro Watanuki's eyes were at the front of his head, and his field of vision naturally did not allow him to see behind him. When someone spoke to him from behind, it was impossible to see who had spoken without turning around. Watanuki was not the sort of high school student who liked being spoken to from behind, but neither was he the type to get worked up about it, so, naturally, he turned around.

There stood a tall, flashy-looking young man Watanuki had never seen before, holding out a thick wallet of luridly colored snakeskin. Watanuki had no more seen the wallet before than he had the young man.

"Um . . . that isn't mine."

"Oh?" the young man said, his head lolling unsettlingly to one side. He slowly looked down at the wallet, and said, very deliberately, "Oh! Oh, right."

Then he looked back at Watanuki and smiled.

"This is *my* wallet."

". . . . ."

"That means I must have been the one that dropped it."

The young man spun the wallet around in his hand and shoved it into his back pocket. Watanuki blinked at him, at a complete loss.

What the hell?

"But you're remarkably free of greed. I was holding the wallet out to you, so you could have just taken it."

"Nah . . . I couldn't have."

Watanuki had a bone or two to pick with the man's choice of second-person pronouns, but Watanuki firmly believed in maintaining manners and civility no matter who he was talking to, and until he could be sure what the man wanted he was not about to broach the subject. He was having enough trouble figuring out how to respond as it was.

"You are a good boy," the man said, obviously mocking him. "You'll definitely go to heaven when you die. You want to go there that badly? Getting into heaven your whole goal in life? You'd do anything to get into heaven. You greedy bastard."

Watanuki was speechless. He'd gone from being remarkably free of greed to being a greedy bastard in the space of a breath. The man's lung capacity was astonishing.

"There was one and a half million yen in that wallet! Or, oh! I see . . . you saw how much money there was and pussied out."

"I wouldn't even take one yen that didn't belong to me.

---

* *Second-person pronouns*   Japanese has many of these, and it is usually considered polite to avoid using any of them with strangers. *Omae,* which the young man uses, is a perfectly ordinary pronoun used by men when speaking to friends, but the use of it could be a little coarse with someone you don't know.

And that is a perfectly normal response," Watanuki said, remembering something his employer was fond of saying. He could not accept anything, even money, that did not come with a fair price, with some payment on his part.

"Hmph. So naive! I hate naive kids. People who cry over one yen also laugh over one!"

"Huh."

Sounded rather hopeful.

"Mm? Did I get that wrong? Was it Kansai people who laugh over one yen while people in Kanto cry over one? Or do I have Kansai and Kanto mixed up? Hmm . . . I think I'm losing track of my point. Japanese is such a difficult language. Ah, doesn't matter. It's all a waste. I'm getting bored. And irritated."

"Uh-huh . . ."

So what?

"I'm about as annoyed as when I'm at work and someone calls my cell and first thing they say is, 'Were you sleeping?' "

"Um . . ."

Even more "so what"?

"Forget it. The more I talk the more annoyed I am. Could not be more annoyed! Never show yourself before me again, high school boy! Get the hell off to school, you little creep."

With that final insult, the man turned his back on Watanuki and wafted away. He was around the corner a moment later, and out of Watanuki's field of vision.

Out of sight.

"Well . . . I guess crazy people don't only come out in spring."

He felt as if the man had been uncommonly rude, but the encounter had been so entirely pointless that Watanuki could not be bothered to get angry. He settled for turning back the way he had originally been headed, and resumed walking. Who, exactly, the man had been was a complete mystery, but he had said one thing that Watanuki could both understand and agree with. Go to school. Yes. Watanuki had, in fact, been on his way there.

To school.

"So much for my good mood . . ." he muttered, hurrying. He had been running late already, even before the man had stopped him. It was certainly unfair, but if he was late it would still be his fault. He knew he should have left earlier, but there was no point in thinking about that now. No point in regretting his choices. When Watanuki had left home he had been unable to predict that he would have a run-in with a strange young man, and there was no point in angrily glaring back at himself reading the horoscope an hour before. His lucky item was *Hojicha*, which was a stroke of luck indeed. Of course, Watanuki's Aries was ranked eighth for the day, but if the run-in with the young man had been the result of that, eighth place did not seem so bad.

"Hmm," Watanuki thought. "Why *was* I in a good mood?"

He had rather absently said "so much for my good mood," the words flowing out naturally, but what good mood? Watanuki was not so skilled at finding small happiness to have responded to being ranked eighth on the daily horoscope, and he did not put much stock in astrology to begin with. He had not even bothered to have a cup of his lucky item, *Hojicha*.

* *Horoscope*   Japanese horoscopes tend to be a bit more involved than the ones in U.S. newspapers. Lucky items are common, as is ranking from luckiest to least lucky.

* *Hojicha*   A kind of Japanese tea where the leaves are roasted over charcoal.

And really . . .

With his eyes . . .

Watanuki did not often find himself in anything that could be called a "good mood."

"What's wrong with me? It's not even spring," he muttered, arriving at school.

He was not late, but the warning bell was already ringing, so he quickly entered the building, bounded up one flight of stairs, and headed for class. As he entered the classroom through the rear doors, someone said, "Good morning!"

It was Sekô Serizawa, the classmate who had dumped a load of trouble in Watanuki's lap on a flimsy age-related excuse. That trouble had been effortlessly cleared away by Watanuki's employer, but ever since, Serizawa had been coming over to him rather often. Watanuki did not particularly consider them friends, and was a little bit thrown by these overtures, but he had not been brought up to harbor ill feelings of anyone named Serizawa, so he had been chatting with him just long enough to avoid seeming rude. If Serizawa said, "Good morning," he would answer in kind.

"Yeah, good morning . . . um," Watanuki said, looking over Serizawa's shoulder at the surprisingly empty classroom. The bell was about to ring, but half the desks were still vacant. Even discounting people who were always late, this was a little alarming. Serizawa clearly knew what Watanuki's shocked expression meant.

"Yeah," he said. "Must be a bug going around. The flu or something."

"This time of year? And so suddenly, without any warning?"

"That we noticed."

"I suppose it *is* possible . . ." Watanuki said, sitting down. He took his books out of his bag and put them in his desk. First period was math. His seat number and the date meant he stood little chance of being called on today, but if class started with this many people absent, all that went out the window. He needed to review quickly.

He glanced sideways.

Empty.

Himawari Kunogi's seat was empty.

No bag next to it, so it seemed she wasn't at school today—she was usually here thirty minutes before the bell rang. It was not like her. Himawari-chan was never late, never absent, and had never gone home sick.

If Himawari-chan was absent, how could he be in a good mood?

Annoyed, he looked out the window.

Looked.

Saw.

"Oh . . ."

At last it dawned on him.

The reason he'd been in a good mood all day.

No, not in a good mood—happy.

Why had he been happy?

"Oh . . . I haven't seen *any* today . . ."

■ ■ ■ ■

Let me quickly review the basic construction of the human eye. Based on common ideas about how vision works, I imagine you have a tendency to confuse the eye with the optic nerves, but in this case, what we mean by "eye"

excludes the optic nerves and the eye muscles. ████████████
████████████████████████████.

25 mm diameter.

Mass of 7.5 g.

The white of the eye is called the sclera, while the cornea covers the colored part. Beneath the sclera is the choroid, and below that the retina, for a three-layered construction, while the cornea has five layers. The sclera and the cornea together form a sphere. Just as there needs to be air inside a tennis ball to make it a sphere, the eye has something called the vitreous humor, which helps it withstand pressure from the outside. There are two types of cells in the retina, called cones and rods. There is a lens, which, along with the cornea, fulfills the same function as a camera lens, and in front of that lens is the pupil, which controls the amount of light allowed to enter the eye. ████, ████████████. All of this is in a junior high school science textbook, but it always helps to look over what we learned as children in the new light maturity brings. From this information alone, it should be much easier for you to understand the Eye World theory.

████████████████████████.

  ████, ████████████████ ████████ ████████████████
████████████████████████ ████████████████.

To proceed, I would like to consider that which our eyes capture—that which we *think* our eyes capture—namely, light. If you feel this is unnecessary, please ignore. ████████████. But even then, we must never cease to think.

Light is a kind of electromagnetic wave. Wavelengths between 7.8×10^{-7}m to 3.8×10^{-7}m are considered visible light: as the name suggests, light we can see, light the human eye is capable of perceiving. Let me just list the full range of the electromagnetic spectrum: radio waves, infrared waves, visible light, ultraviolet waves, X-rays, and gamma rays. Occasionally the rest of these are referred to as nonvisible light, but this should be viewed as a mere colloquialism. There are, after all, species with eyes that can perceive infrared and ultraviolet rays. ██████, ████████████. You can break each type of ray down into still more detailed types, but if we go down that road we'll never get out of this tangent, so I shall reluctantly refrain.

According to modern science, the spirits that ████████'s eyes perceive are defined as dwelling within X-rays or gamma rays. But according to the Eye World theory I propose, the spirits ████████ sees are more likely to be in the longer wave range. In neither instance would they normally be perceived by humans, but that wavelength is critical to my theory. *Theory* might be a bold word for it, but I believe I can demonstrate that it is far closer to reality than earlier ideas.

Light is a wave; but it is also particles.

It has component parts.

And before I proceed to explain my theories further, I would like to once again emphasize the quality of light that is most critical to the understanding thereof: that light can be refracted.

And anything that refracts cannot be captured directly.

■ ■ ■ ■

The day's curriculum completed without difficulty, Kimihiro Watanuki left the grounds of Cross Private School and headed to the nearest shopping area. He planned to make *nabe* for dinner that evening and needed supplies. His employer had not specified exactly what the *nabe* should contain, so Watanuki had decided on duck. And while he was at it, he

---

° *Nabe*   A meal cooked in a large pot at the center of the table. Duck (*kamo*—same kanji as in Serizawa Kamo) *nabe* involves duck, *hakusai* (Chinese cabbage), tofu, and *negi* (scallions/green onions).

might as well pick up some *Hojicha*. He was sure there was a decent tea store in that area.

By the end of the day, a fair amount of the seats had been occupied, with a number of students arriving late. But many seats remained empty, and Himawari Kunogi's was one of those. About eighty percent of Watanuki's motivation for going to school was seeing Himawari-chan's face, so this left him rather dejected.

Or should have.

"But . . ."

There was a very big *but*.

He could not see spirits.

Not one.

None.

No matter how far he looked, he could not see a thing.

This was the first time this had ever happened to Watanuki. No matter what condition he was in, no matter what situation he found himself facing, he had never gone this long without seeing any spirits.

He felt light, as light as his emotions.

As though he was wearing someone else's shell.

His body, his mind, every cell in his body felt as though it had been released from its bonds. In other words, he was in a good mood. Himawari's absence was in a completely different dimension . . .

However.

"Out of the blue like this . . . I'm more confused than happy. What's going on?"

Other than the fact that he could see no spirits, Watanuki's eyes appeared to be functioning normally. Not a thing unusual, nothing out of place. But that just made it more baffling. Spirits were always there, always around—it was just the way of Watanuki's world. For them to suddenly vanish . . . what could it mean?

Serizawa and his other classmates didn't know about Watanuki's eyes . . . so there was no one he could talk to about this. The only person in school he could share it with was the president of the next class, an individual who would undoubtedly look like some sort of green dog if he were in an anime based on a work by Shigeru Mizuki,* but when Watanuki had gone to see him at lunch he had been absent, much like Himawari Kunogi.

This must be what they call the demon's sunstroke.*

Well. It might be a little unsettling, but if he asked his employer, she would clear everything up. He had no idea how much he would have to pay her for that, but what else could he do? The price would be fair; with Yûko Ichihara, it always was.

Kimihiro Watanuki's job.

At the shop where wishes were granted.

The shop owned by Yûko Ichihara.

"If I make a good *nabe* and put her in a good mood she might clear things up for free. At any rate, I can't be comfortable unless I know why this happened. Can't quite decide how I should react to this . . ."

He finished his shopping and headed directly to the shop.

---

* *Shigeru Mizuki*   Creator of *Gegege no Kitaro* and many other works dealing with Japanese *yokai* (apparitions or spirits).

* *Demon's sunstroke*   Literal translation of *oni no kakuran*, a Japanese idiom used when a normally healthy person gets sick.

It had taken longer to pick out the ingredients than he thought, but he should still be on time.

Even so.

As Watanuki walked, he looked ahead of him.

No matter what you were thinking about, you had to look ahead of you when you walked—and there were no spirits in front of him.

Things that had naturally been there . . .

. . . were now naturally not.

Not seeing spirits made him realize just how much a part of his daily life they were. And despite his good mood, he was a little nervous.

He stopped, and looked up.

The sky.

White clouds—blinding sun.

Clear blue sky.

Ordinary things.

But he had never seen the sky like this. To Watanuki, the sky was the spirits' domain, their nest, and it was never clear blue but always dirty blue. An empty sky was one of the least likely things in the world. Clouds and the sun were just the background for spirits. He had never been able to gaze peacefully upon the stars. In fact, the number of spirits increased dramatically at night. Even people with no interest in astrology could find the Big Dipper and Orion, but through the spirit filter he could barely make them out. Which meant his elementary school field trip to an observatory had been a nightmare.

He looked down again, and then all around him. Checking everything there was to be seen.

Then . . .

"Wow . . . the world . . ."

———

The world was so big.

———

He had mixed feelings about this.

Partly he just didn't know how to react to this situation, partly he was still flustered by not knowing what had caused it—but there was an even bigger reason.

Namely, the idea that there was no one in the world who could understand the way he felt.

Watanuki had just looked up at the sky and marveled at its beauty. But to anyone with normal eyes, it was just the boring old sky, nothing special at all. It seemed likely that nobody on earth but Watanuki would have felt anything looking at this sky. It was just part of everyday life. The world Watanuki felt was so very big was just a narrow back road to anyone else.

But so what?

Was he really that petty?

The more tiny things stopped him in his tracks, the more he sat down in places ordinary people would have brushed on past, the more he looked around him in wonder . . . the more he felt like he was torturing himself.

Something was wrong, he realized belatedly.

The road from school to work was one he walked every day, part of his routine, and he was often lost in thought as he walked it, as he had been today.

Which is why he hadn't noticed.

He couldn't see the walls.

Those black walls.

Those black walls that surrounded the shop where Watanuki worked like magical wards, those black walls that seemed
to suck you into the shop where wishes were granted . . . he
couldn't see them. He should have been able to the second he
started down this back road, but . . .

"Huh . . . ? What the . . . ?"

His pace quickened, helplessly.

Even as his mind was reeling, he had to know for sure.
Even though he already did, somewhere deep inside . . . it
was clear, so very clear, beyond all doubt. Beyond all capacity to deny. Conviction bordering on the unshakable. But he
had to check anyway.

With his own eyes.

He had to see.

———

". . . Yûko-san."

———

The place where Kimihiro Watanuki worked.

The shop where wishes were granted.

The place where it should have been . . . had become a
flashily decorated hundred-yen shop.

■ ■ ■ ■

Despite this, the Eye World theory does not have such a violent personality that it would flatly deny all of modern science—although I cannot deny that a part of it does. ████████████. In other words, it just looks that way since the bulk of its framework is composed of original theories. No matter how obvious or sensible what I'm saying is, if all the ideas are my own creation, it ends up looking dubious, and I fully understand the perception that I'm making it all up to defy the prevailing wisdom. ████████. That part of it will need to be independently verified. An absolute must. ████████████. This will be like debugging: a time-consuming slog. Obviously, work is continuing even while I'm here. In that sense, nothing I can say here is at all definite.

But this is one thing I can say for sure.

The Eye World theory does not deny your worldviews.

It may deny the world itself, but even as it does, it accepts your worldviews.

As you know, humans possess five senses: sight, hearing, taste, sense of smell, and sense of touch. These senses allow us to perceive and define the world. But these five senses are not operating in a balanced and fair fashion. They are uneven, weighted. Quite honestly, 90 percent of human perception of the world is based on sight. The four remaining senses have to divide up the remaining 10 percent between them. Of course, there is the entirely groundless idea of a sixth sense, but at this point we shall be ignoring that. ████████████████████████. We shall consider this in depth later, but in principle, the Eye World theory deals with the normal five senses.

For example, if there were something here that allowed you to perceive the world as if you could reach out and touch it, you would not actually be able to reach out and touch it; it would only look as if you could. Only 90 percent of your senses would be telling you that you could.

It would just look like it.

But just seeing is often enough.

██, ████, ████████████

███████████

███████

It also allows us to perceive distance, a faculty worth stressing here. In order to perceive the size of the world, we need our eyes, with their ability to perceive a third dimension and perspective. But, as I hardly need to point out, there is a significant discrepancy between the actual world and the world as our eyes perceive it. We could even call it a paradox. The cables that convey only the information our eyes provide to the encephalon—the optic nerves—are not nearly powerful enough to handle the job. ████████████████. If we were to attempt to transmit all the information the eyes receive to the brain without any loss or deficit, the optic nerves would need to be as thick as the arm of the average adult male. Even if that were possible, we have no way of telling if the encephalon actually has the hard memory required to process it. The human brain is certainly capable of processing a great deal of information, but there is no guarantee that it would be enough to perceive the entirety of the world.

I'm sure you understand by now.

I am stressing the importance of the eyes.

I would not even object to the extreme assertion that all human functions exist subordinate to the eyes. The world of the eyes is absolute, superior to everything else. ████████████. They occupy 90 percent of the balance, so we could even call it democratic.

The Eye World theory.

██, ███████████████████,

███████████████████████,

██████████████. Certainly, it sounds comical, and if one were to try and construct a theory by conventional procedures it would be a dangerous hypothesis that could only be dismissed as childish scribbles, but ████████, ████, ████████

██████████████
██████████████

By this time I am sure you are all tired of hearing me speak about it in general terms, so let me get back to the story of when I directly encountered the boy with the strange, sinister, and utterly unique world in his eyes, █████████. The boy who could see spirits. I am sure you have not forgotten, but it is absolutely essential that you remember that he did not at all consider this a desirable state to be in.

But that was the state he was in.

Regardless of his own opinion.

Regardless of his own desires.

■ ■ ■ ■

Not at all sure where to go, but not yet ready to go home, Watanuki wandered aimlessly, still carrying the bag of *nabe* supplies. Eventually he found himself in the park with a fountain, where he'd resolved the problem Serizawa had brought him. He had no particular affection for this park, but he happened to pass it just as he was getting tired from walking around. "Happened"—pure coincidence. Since his employer was not where she should be to insist that there was no coincidence every time he carelessly used the word, then perhaps he *should* use it. The *nabe* supplies, duck included, were all perishable, and he needed to get them put away as soon as possible, but at the moment he just couldn't bring himself to care.

He sat down on a bench.

On the same animal-shaped bench he'd sat on the last time he was here.

He had once heard that sitting alone on a park bench made you seem like a sad, lonely individual hopelessly waiting for someone, but that didn't matter to him now. Who was there to wait for, anyway?

After what he'd seen.

The hundred-yen shop.

The shop where things of little value gather, his employer had called it.

"I knew . . . at least, I thought that something like this might happen, but still . . ." he whispered . . . muttered under his breath.

But if what had happened was what Watanuki suspected, then perhaps he should not be complaining. It was like harboring suspicions, finding faults, picking fights, making excuses, leveling false charges. No matter who those actions were directed against, he could never be proud of them.

After all . . .

If he was right, then this was what Kimihiro Watanuki had always wanted.

———

To not see.

———

He had wished for it every single day.

And he had slaved under Yûko Ichihara to get that wish granted . . . only to get that wish granted.

In the hour and a half it had taken him to get here from the hundred-yen shop that had replaced Yûko's shop, he had not seen a single spirit. At this point there was only one conclusion he could draw. No—this was something he should have thought of right away, in class, when he realized he had not seen any spirits.

In other words . . .

Watanuki had paid his fair price.

Kimihiro Watanuki's wish had come true.

Watanuki's eyes could no longer perceive spirits.

He had been working at the shop where wishes were granted . . .

. . . and his wish had been granted.

He was in a good mood, his body felt light, his feelings felt light, and the reason for all of that could be explained so easily. So very easily. Not only could he no longer see them, the spirits drawn to the blood in his body were no longer attracted to him. And one thing proved that to him more than anything.

Shizuka Dômeki.

President of the class next to his, the boy Watanuki had gone to for advice when he discovered he had not seen any spirits. Sadly, he had been absent, and Watanuki had been unable to ask anything, but the very fact that he had been disappointed to find him absent was terrifyingly unnatural — after all, Watanuki hated Dômeki like a snakepit. He would rather swim through a pool filled with snakes than ask Dômeki's help on anything.

Except . . . he had been disappointed.

He had gone to him for advice.

According to Yûko, the reason Watanuki hated Dômeki so much was also because of spirits. Shizuka Dômeki was the heir to an exorcist, and despite not being able to see any spirits he was congenitally, subconsciously able to drive them away. So the spirits after Watanuki's blood had concocted a great many schemes and strategies to keep Watanuki away from Dômeki. Watanuki could get irritable just thinking about Dômeki, and this explanation made a lot of sense to him. Not that it changed anything . . .

But those feelings had vanished entirely.

Without even thinking about it, he had gone to ask him for help.

"Spirits . . . ?"

If he could no longer see them . . . wasn't that a good thing?

Shouldn't he be happy?

If he could be around Shizuka Dômeki without seething with meaningless rage, then hooray. Nothing to gripe about there. Given their relationship until the day before, he couldn't simply change his attitude instantly like the flip of a coin, but Watanuki already found himself wondering what he had ever had against him. Getting to know him better seemed like a dandy idea.

He should be happy.

The world was so big.

So beautiful.

Wasn't that just great?

The fact that he could not share these thoughts and feelings with anyone was a minor detail. Who cared? He could think about that later, at his leisure. For now he should simply rejoice.

Still.

Despite all this . . .

"A hundred-yen shop? Come on, Yûko-san! That's a little low! Like some sort of twisted joke! I mean, it is very much your style, but . . ."

Yûko Ichihara . . . had vanished.

Shop and all.

Walls and all.

Completely, without a trace, like a soap bubble.

Which was also very much her style.

Come to think of it, Yûko had explained that hers was the shop where wishes were granted . . . and people with no wishes to be granted could not even enter it. He had laughed it off as her usual moontalk, but perhaps she had not been joking. He should have listened more carefully. It had never occurred to him that the shop might vanish completely.

But perhaps that did not really matter that much. If his wish was granted, then his wish was no more, and even if the shop had still been there, now that his wish had been granted there was no reason for Watanuki to keep going there. Once his goal was met, there was no reason for him to suffer that horrible and unproductive job.

He had never wanted that job.

He had just ended up with it.

Still . . .

"Still . . . I would have liked to thank you, Yûko-san . . ."

She could have eaten the *nabe*.

She could have said goodbye.

It wasn't as though he was reluctant to part, it wasn't as though there was anything drawing him back there . . . and it definitely wasn't as though he had ever felt any great affection for Yûko. He knew full well how coldhearted she was. But even so . . . he would have liked her to be a little more considerate.

"Man, I sound like such a sap . . ."

Even though the sky was this beautiful.

Even though his wish had been granted.

Why was he so . . .

———

"I found this wallet."

———

This time he did not need to turn around.

Because the voice came from right in front of him.

There stood a tall, flashy-looking young man holding out a thick wallet of luridly colored snakeskin. Neither of which Watanuki had ever seen before.

No.

He had seen them.

This morning.

"Um . . . that isn't mine."

"Oh?" The young man frowned, and slowly looked down at the wallet. "Oh, right, right," he said, comprehension dawning. Then he looked at Watanuki, and smiled.

"This is my wallet."

Watanuki waited.

"Except it isn't really mine. Then whose is it? Who gives a damn? You shouldn't stick your damn nose in other people's business, retard. Drop dead, asshole."

On this last invective, the man hauled back his arm, and before Watanuki even had time to think *No way,* he had flung the wallet into the garbage receptacle next to the bench. The wallet containing (if the man was to be believed) 1.5 million yen hit the receptacle hard and buried itself beneath a pile of empty soda cans.

"Sigh . . . okay, all right," he said, settling down next to Watanuki. Disregarding the minor sitting next to him, he produced a cigarette and lit it.

In what was undoubtedly a completely normal reaction, Watanuki took offense at the man's attitude. He was hardly in the mood for dealing with the sort of person who could see the schoolboy he'd made fun of that morning sitting on a park bench and come over to make fun of him again. No amount of effort on Watanuki's part would leave him feeling amenable to dealing with some off-season eccentric.

Avoiding the man's eyes, he silently rose to leave. He was not yet ready to head home, but that was no reason to hang around this park under these conditions.

But then the man said, "Don't be in such a hurry, Kimihiro Watanuki."

"Huh?" Watanuki said, feeling his eyes narrow. He glared at the man, who smiled back at him. An extremely phony smile. A smile that could not be mistaken for genuine.

And this man's eyes . . .

. . . were unsettling, somehow.

"Did I tell you my name?"

"Your name? Come now, you're not the kind of person who needs to do that. It's as though you started handing out business cards the day you were born! You ought to know just how famous you are, really. Trying to pretend you're ordinary? What a prick."

Watanuki was speechless.

He remembered being told something very much like this once before . . . but that time he had been speaking with a spirit, not a human. And no matter how strange this man might be, no matter how unsettling his eyes were, he was no spirit . . . he was human.

"Or do you just not like having me address you by name?

Already decided to hate me? Can't say I blame you. People always hate me the first time they meet me."

Being hated by everyone you meet seemed like a fairly significant flaw for a human to have, but this situation lacked the warmth and comfort required to dwell on such trivialities.

"But Watanuki is a good name, Watanuki. Watanuki, Watanuki, Watanuki."

"A good name? It's just hard to read."

"Oh? But Kimihiro's good, right? Like I'm asking you something . . . what am I asking? Mm? Watanuki. Ha! Don't make me laugh."

"And your name?" he asked, convinced he was wasting his time. By this point he was sure he was dealing with the sort of person who refuses to give out their real name. Because knowledge of one's real name meant you could touch their soul. The question did little besides buy Watanuki a little time.

"My name?" the man said, lightly, openly, with no resistance. "My name is Basara Bakemachi. The noted physicist."

" . . . . "

"My more gossipy friends call me a genius, but you can call me whatever you like. I'm one hundred eighty-eight centimeters tall, seventy-seven kilograms—as you can see, tall, thin, and bad-ass. My personality is god-awful, much too antagonistic, but I have my adorable side, so watch closely. Born on November eleventh, which makes me a Scorpio, and my blood type is O. No family—alone in the world. My eyes

---

° *Watanuki*   Written with the kanji for "April 1." Most people would not know how to pronounce the name without being told.

° *Kimihiro*   Written with the kanji for "you" and "ask."

are twenty-twenty—hmm? What is it, Watanuki? I'm busy introducing myself, and here you are looking like a pigeon shot with a peashooter."

"Um . . . I did ask, but I didn't think you'd actually give your name."

"Ha! Only a coward hides his true name," he spat.

That . . . was certainly true.

But not the point.

"What . . ." Watanuki asked, making up his mind.

Nothing would ever make sense otherwise. If he knew Watanuki's name, then this strange young man who called himself Basara Bakemachi, noted physicist, was clearly not just an off-season lunatic. But that did not change the fact that Watanuki did not want to deal with someone like him in his current state of mind.

As Bakemachi had said, he had been in a hurry, trying to clear everything away as quickly as possible.

"What do you want with me?"

"Isn't it fricking obvious?" Bakemachi said. "I hear you've got these amazing eyes."

He had said Watanuki was famous.

That meant it was no surprise that Bakemachi knew about his eyes. In fact, it would have been quite strange if he had not. By this point it mattered little exactly how he knew.

Nevertheless . . .

"I don't know who you are, but you shouldn't call the source of all one's worry 'amazing.' "

He had to say it.

---

* *Off-season lunatic* Literally meaning out of season, untimely.

Out of all the possible things it was possible to say, this was the one Watanuki least wanted anyone to say to him. His ability to see what should not be seen had never once done anything positive for him. If praising other people's flaws was *moe* — Yûko had said something like that, and it seemed apt — it was still not something the object of it wanted to hear. It was like someone incessantly poking at a festering wound with evident fascination.

"Some things are just amazing, Watanuki. I mean, you can see spirits! If that isn't amazing, what is? If that isn't a talent, what is? Huh? Some sort of roundabout bragging going on here? That'd make you a lot more of a creep than you look."

Bakemachi's tone made it clear he could not give a damn what Watanuki's thoughts on the subject were.

"Talent . . . ? Just doesn't sound right . . ."

"Why the hell don't you use that talent for the good of the world? Why don't you even try to use it? Are you just that frigging lazy!?"

"Of all the selfish — Do you have any idea how much I've suffered because of these eyes?"

"Nobody wants to hear a genius whine," Bakemachi sneered, dismissively. He was not laughing; he looked genuinely angry. "You really are a prick. There's a nasty taste in my mouth, and it's because of you. If you think acting all humble makes you look good, Watanuki, you're an idiot. Only the mediocre are allowed to go through life praising modesty and restraint. If you can't handle your own talent, then that's no one's fault but your own! Wallow in self-pity as much as you like, make all the excuses you can, but don't ever say that crap aloud! The last thing anyone with real talent should do for someone without it is be *modest*. The last thing! Those with power can pretend to have no power, but all it does is piss off anyone who doesn't have that power!"

"I didn't mean to . . ."

"I hate people who say naive crap, but I hate people who make naive excuses even more. You just haven't faced up to yourself."

All Watanuki could do was wonder why he had to get treated like this by a man he didn't know and had only just met. Bakemachi's words had no other effect on him. He could understand the idea, and he knew what the man was trying to say. But regardless of how right or wrong Bakemachi might be, he could not stand to have his eyes talked about like this.

"So what if my eyes are amazing? That doesn't have anything to do with you!"

"Huh? What, other people can't get involved? Long as you're alive, they will be. Just being alive means you get mixed up in other people's business all the time. Can't stop yourself. Wait . . . did I say the opposite a moment ago? I forget. Never mind. Point is, you ought to join my group."

"Group?"

"Yeah. Unlike making friends and lovers, you can join a group just by deciding to do so. Just got to turn and face the same direction. Helps if we all got skills in common."

"Common?"

A group.

That was a word that sounded very strange, coming from Bakemachi. He seemed like the kind of guy who'd been born not giving a damn if he fit into any kind of group.

But even so . . .

Bakemachi had said the word.

"I call it the Eye World theory," Bakemachi said. "It's a theory I . . . no, *we're* proposing. To simplify it, it's based on the idea that our eyes *are* the world—a new idea nobody else in history has ever come up with. If you want to join my group, Watanuki, we'll be able to treat your eyes as a very useful sample."

"Eye . . . World theory?"

"And don't you forget it."

"In other words, you want to use my eyes for something? In that case, Bakemachi . . . san, Bakemachi-san, I'm sorry. I don't know what sort of theory that is, but I'm simply not interested, and frankly, you're a little late. Yesterday I might have been able to help, but now . . . my eyes don't see spirits anymore," Watanuki said.

Did not see—did not perceive.

He could look all around the park without seeing a single spirit, only the mysterious man who kept bothering him.

"My eyes no longer—"

"Wow, that is . . . a very special kind of brain you have there. Are you capable of comprehending the world only in a way that benefits yourself? Have you never even stopped to think just how great a world those eyes behind your glasses are supporting? How can a world like that just up and vanish? There's no reason on earth why you should stop being able to see what you've been able to see all this time."

"B-but . . . I . . ."

He really couldn't see anything. This guy was just babbling on without knowing what he was talking about. Bakemachi spat out his cigarette and ground it into the dirt.

Apparently he was not the type to be bothered by littering regulations.

"Yûko Ichihara?"

"Eh . . . ?"

Watanuki could not hide his surprise at the name. Did . . . did the man know Yûko? That would explain Bakemachi's weird mean streak . . .

"You know her?"

"Huh? *Her?* Sorry, the Ichihara I know ain't something I'd be willing to define as human. Probably not even as a living thing. We consider Yûko Ichihara and everything inside those black walls an external concept, an alternative state of being."

Apparently . . . he did know her.

Although it was hard to describe his opinion of her as favorable.

"Watanuki, you sound as though you put a lot of trust in Ichihara, so I'm sorry to pull the rug out from under you. Really. You can't see spirits? And you thought that was because of Yûko Ichihara?"

"You say otherwise?"

"I do," Bakemachi nodded. "It's because of me."

"Huh? What do you have to do . . . did you do something to me?"

"Course I did. I'm a *dôjutsu* master, obviously. Twit."

"*Dôjutsu* . . . . . ?"

---

* *You know her?*   The Japanese Watanuki uses literally translates as "that person." It's a perfectly normal way to refer to someone in Japanese, but a little too awkward to use in English. Bakemachi is objecting to Watanuki's assertion that Yûko is human.

* *Dôjutsu*   Pupil/eye technique.

"Nobody would ever come up with anything like the Eye World theory unless their own eyes were abnormal. You got to know what you're talking about. You ought to try thinking sometimes, Watanuki. Or did you think you were the main character in a tragedy?"

At this turn of phrase, Watanuki could not stop himself from meeting Bakemachi's eyes. His eyes . . . eyeballs, pupils. This was the first time he'd ever looked right into Bakemachi's eyes, and he instantly wanted to look away.

Wished he'd never looked.

The man's eyes were very . . . abnormal.

Well beyond "unsettling."

"Then . . . you mean, Bakemachi-san . . . you can see spirits too?"

"Yeah. There's lots of kinds of abnormal eyes. The kind you have, that can see spirits, is called *kenki*. But I can see a lot more than just spirits—I can also see *mayakashi*."

"*Mayakashi?*"

"*Ayakashi* . . . and *mayakashi*."

Bakemachi opened his eyes wide.

As though he saw something on Watanuki's face.

"My right eye can see spirits . . . and my left eye sees deceit. Your eyes are amazing . . . but mine are more amazing. But it doesn't really matter that I can see more than you. I'm a rank higher than you on the abnormal charts, but we have the same eyes. What really matters here is that I know how to use my *kenki* eyes. I have mastered my abil-

---

° *Mayakashi*   Deception, fraud, fake.

° *Ayakashi*   This is the word we usually translate as "spirits."

ity to see spirits and deceit. In other words, I am alive, but it is like I am dead; I am human, but it is like I'm a spirit — I'm a monster in my own right. Wherever I go, spirits get out of my way."

"Spirits . . . avoid you?"

No way, that couldn't be — No. No, there was no reason why not . . . Watanuki already knew someone like that. The president of the class next to his, Shizuka Dômeki. The grandson of an exorcist, he could not see any spirits, but the blood flowing through his veins was enough to ensure that spirits never came near him. Which proved spirits could detect danger and avoid it. If Watanuki's eyes and blood attracted them, then the opposite could also be true.

Which meant the reason Watanuki had not seen any spirits that day was not because his eyes could no longer see them. . . .

"Because you're here?"

"Yeah. Because I'm here." Bakemachi took out a new cigarette, adding, "They scatter like baby spiders. More sensitive humans will avoid me too, instinctively, unconsciously. Because I can see deceit as well as spirits. The more someone keeps hidden inside, the more I see. Like I said, people always hate me the first time they meet me."

"People?"

Oh . . . Watanuki remembered the empty classroom, all those absent people. Even Himawari Kunogi and Shizuka Dômeki had been absent. And . . . that was also because of Bakemachi.

"Basara Bakemachi, hated more than anything or anyone. All it takes is me wandering by and *poof*, the whole town's like this. This is how *dôjutsu* was meant to be used, Watanuki."

Watanuki was silent.

Dômeki's ability to keep spirits away was fairly impressive . . . but it couldn't affect the entire town. They weren't even worth comparing. If what Bakemachi said was true, his eyes were very powerful indeed.

It almost sounded . . . like deceit.

"But even though you have *kenki* eyes, and your sensitivity is way beyond everyone else's . . . you're here talking to me. And that, more than anything else, is proof you have not mastered your *dôjutsu*. Right now, you're nothing but a lazy bastard wasting the gift you were born with."

"I . . ." Watanuki stammered, not sure what to say.

The same eyes.

Someone other than him . . . with the same eyes.

Even if Watanuki's eyes could see spirits, if there were no spirits, there was nothing to see. The power in Bakemachi's eyes was enough to drive the spirits away. And he was saying that Watanuki would be able to do the same thing if he learned to use them properly . . . but . . .

"I never really wanted these eyes."

"Forget that! Search the whole world, you won't find anyone living a life that consists only of things they want. You only need things you want? Most people have all kinds of things they don't want and can't get rid of and all kinds of things they do want but can't have, but they all keep right on living. You're no different from anyone else, in that respect."

"But I . . ."

"Do you know just how many factors had to come into

play for you to get those eyes? Do you know just what wind-ing path fate had to take? Just how miraculous they are? Do you think you received those eyes for no reason at all? And yet you're going to Ichihara, trying to throw those eyes away. Trying to damage what you got from your parents. Don't you think that's pathetic? Don't you have any pride at all? That's as sad as finding a bunch of money but getting all scared and throwing the lot in a ditch somewhere. Pure cowardice."

The wallet he'd thrown in the trash receptacle.

The cigarette he'd ground under his feet.

"The kind of coward who wouldn't cash in a winning lot-tery ticket."

"Y-you don't understand anything, Bakemachi-san. You don't understand!" His voice shook.

Not because he was rattled. He was, but not only because of that. Mostly because he was absolutely furious.

"All the pain these eyes have caused me . . . everything I've put up with . . ."

"Put up with? Why didn't you try to get over it?" Bakemachi sneered.

A pitying sort of sneer.

"If you really mean that, then you're more than a coward—you're downright craven. Disguising the truth with words that just *sound* good. Turning your eyes from reality. Shoulder it! It is *your* burden!"

"Th-that's why I went to Yûko-san!"

Yûko-san . . .

Right, where was she? He could understand why Kunogi and Dômeki would have hidden themselves when they sensed Bakemachi and his left eye, the one that saw deceit, but why would Yûko vanish . . . taking her shop with her? Kunogi and Dômeki were ordinary humans, but she was nothing like them. Or were Bakemachi's eyes just that powerful? Powerful enough to defeat Yûko Ichihara? No. No, that wasn't true. Bakemachi refused to define Yûko as human . . . in which case . . .

In which case . . . why?

"Ichihara? That's what pisses me off the most! Why are you leaving it up to someone else, Watanuki? They're your eyes! You're eyes aren't good for nothing—they're your eyes! Why would you go to someone else to solve this? Sure, some people might want to unload a talent that was too much for them—people think different things. But if you're gonna unload them, why not do it yourself? Don't make other people take out your trash!"

"I didn't say I was . . . and don't make up things I didn't say! I'm paying a fair price to get my wish granted!"

"Fair price? Those *nabe* supplies next to you count as a fair price? Working for Ichihara counts as a fair price? Don't you think that's sad? Don't you feel any shame? You're used like a slave and you're happy about it if you can't see spirits anymore? Or are you so used to being kept, your very ability to feel has melted away? Come on, Watanuki! What in god's name made you trust Ichihara? What the hell did that *thing* ever do for you?"

"She's . . . Yûko-san has saved me several times! Of course I had to pay a fair price each time, but she . . ."

"Please! Stop calling Ichihara 'she'! If you insist on this delusion that that thing is human, the two of us will never come to an understanding. I may have gone on about you leaving your business to other people, but Ichihara ain't even a person! Augh, I can't believe you're making me say all this again! What? Ichihara saved you? Don't be stupid. Think about it! You'd never have been in trouble in the first place if it weren't for Ichihara, right?"

"W-well . . ."

When he put it that way . . . he had a point.

He was right.

"All the time before you met Yûko Ichihara . . . and less than a year since then. Which was stranger? You might have felt a little less stress since you've dumped your burden in Ichihara's lap; it's always easier when you stop thinking for yourself. It's easy to be tempted away from a hopeless discipline by deceitful hope."

A *deceitful* hope.

"Did you never think? That Ichihara might just be using you? That Ichihara might just be using you? That Ichihara might be exploiting the *kenki* eyes you were born with?"

"Exploiting? That's not . . ."

"Your eyes belong to you! Only you should be using your eyes! Why are you renting them out? Had Ichihara done anything to deserve that? You've been toiling away all this time and your eyes haven't improved one bit! No matter how magnificent their talent, people who abandon their own thoughts and desires spend their entire lives as pet dogs! Woof woof whine? If you looooove Ichihara like that, then let her put a collar on you! Let her take you for a walk while you wag your goddamn tail like a complete and utter moron!"

". . . . . !"

Of all the — How had he ended up getting talked to like

this? Even if everything Bakemachi said made perfect sense, so what? It wasn't bothering him any. Why was Basara Bakemachi berating Kimihiro Watanuki . . . as if he were yelling at himself?

Did Bakemachi have some grudge against him?

"Then what *should* I do?" Watanuki said, unable to stand it any longer. "Think about how I feel! Think about how I felt, having no choice but to rely on Yûko-san! It's not as though I mistook her for a good person, and hell yes, I hate working like a slave for her! I've longed to quit my job countless times! But I don't have any other choice!"

"That's how a loser thinks," Bakemachi snapped, cutting him off. "Like I said, I don't want to hear a genius whine. You aren't allowed to be that indolent. I'm embarrassed just to have the same eyes as you. Listen, Watanuki. There have always been infinite choices. How you felt never had anything to do with it. I never, no matter how wrongheaded I was, would have gone to Ichihara. And not just Ichihara—I would never have gone to anyone. I would have made up my own mind. And that's just normal. Nothing to brag about."

"Then . . ." Watanuki said again, trapped. "What should I do?"

"Help me prove the Eye World theory," Bakemachi said instantly, as if he'd been waiting for this. "Of course, not as a servant or a slave. As part of the group, as one of those with abnormal eyes. As one of those with unusual abilities. You asked me what I wanted to use your eyes for, but I'm not going to do that, not like Ichihara. I won't use them, and I won't use you. I don't need to. I already have the same skills you do. To be strictly accurate, no two sets of abnormal eyes are the same, and there are countless different types, but I'm trying to make a point, not a rebuttal."

His eyes looked into Watanuki's. Those eyes that could see both spirits and deceit.

"Don't throw them away. Learn to use them, Watanuki. Steal that technique from me. The Eye World theory will be to your benefit—at least, much more so than working for Ichihara. The Eye World theory will teach you how to avoid spirits—or at least, how to make them avoid you. The *dôjutsu* of *kenki* eyes is very powerful. You've felt great all day, just because I came to town, right? And you can make that power yours. Drive away everyone who annoys you."

"Everyone?"

"Humans will avoid you too, right?" Bakemachi said, grinning.

Why did Bakemachi spend so much effort attempting to smile? Watanuki wondered, randomly. If he couldn't smile, then he shouldn't. It was as though he was pretending to be human.

Any number of animals can shed tears.

But only humans smile.

"I believe talent is not a right but a duty. It's a fundamental crime to take what you have and stuff it away in a box somewhere never to be used. And a really pathetic crime. Not using something you have without any effort on your part is making a mockery of the world. Are you stupid? Are you? After all I've said, you still haven't realized? All those times Ichihara saved you from messes Ichihara caused, you'd have gotten out of it just fine on your own if you'd known how to use your eyes! If you could use those eyes ... how many other people could you have saved?"

"That's ..."

"And it's *your fault* they weren't saved!" Bakemachi roared. "You're the only person in the world! Everything else is spirits and deceit!"

Watanuki had no answer.

"So you have to take responsibility for yourself!"

Responsibility.

Responsibility for his eyes.

For what he saw—for the act of seeing.

"What you're saying ..."

He was out of breath.

His head spinning.

Spinning ... he felt dizzy.

Who the hell was he talking to? What was he talking about?

"What is this Eye World theory?"

"Mm? Getting interested? Or just dodging the conversational momentum? Doesn't matter. We have no whiteboard and no models, so it's sort of hard for me to explain here, and I seriously doubt you have the makings of a physicist. You might look like a science type, but you tend toward the literary, right? I can tell from the way you talk, trying to make everything all neat and tidy. So typical, everything's got to match your thesis. Let me tell you, no thesis ever stood up to logic. What you need isn't a thesis, but an emotional reaction. Fundamental basis of all good science.

° *Science vs. literary*   The main division between academic disciplines in Japan.

"You have to say stuff that's wild and crazy," Bakemachi added, then paused for a moment.

"Like I said earlier, the Eye World theory means that your eyes are the world. That's the simplest way to understand it. That's all there is to it, that's the ultimate goal of it, there's nothing more to know. But to get to that point, to explain the theory, we need people like you and me, who have *dôjutsu.*"

Eyes . . . were the world.

"Of course, by the world what I really mean is worldview. When I try and explain this without any technical jargon so even stupid people can understand it, I've got an example I like to use, but that example probably makes it harder to understand for someone with abnormal eyes. Anyway, assume I'm talking about a friend, and hear the example out. Watanuki, have you ever seen, like, a bit of string hanging in the air where you know nothing should be?"

"Um . . . yes. And when you turn your eyes it slides away and vanishes?"

"Right. Big joke in *Azumanga Daioh* about that. My favorite character in that manga is Kagura, but who was yours, Watanuki?"

"Stick to the point."

"Not until you answer."

"Then, um, Sakaki-san."

" 'Then, um'? You can't talk about what you like or don't like as if your choice can be replaced! So obvious you're ready to jump ship to Chiyo-chan the moment anything hap-

---

° *Azumanga Daioh*   Manga by Kiyohiko Azuma.

pens to Sakaki-san! As stupid as you are, you have the nerve
to treat me like an idiot? And when stupid people start treat-
ing you like an idiot you must be a real retard. 'Then.' 'Um.'
That whole attitude is just frigging indicative of your innate
cowardice! Anyway. Those things—you can even see them if
you close your eyes. What do you think they are?"

"I think . . . I heard they were distortions in the vitreous
humor. The vitreous humor or the crystalline lens. Not part
of the light entering the eye, but shadows within the eyeball
itself cast on the retina. There's not actually anything in the
air, you're just seeing something in your eye . . ."

"Right, exactly. Helps if you already know—and those
with abnormal eyes have phases of vision normal people
don't have. This example often doesn't make sense to them."

"I'm glad it helps . . . but I still don't see your point."

"You don't see? Apt way of putting it, you don't see my
point. You'll be able to see it soon enough, Watanuki. We can
see things that are inside our eyes. Which means . . . the
world you can see right now might also exist entirely within
your eyes."

". !"

"That's the Eye World theory, dumbo!"

Not "able to see"—simply existing.

Not externally—but internally.

The light—refracted.

"To make you feel that you understood I had to put it sort
of roughly. Those strings you see over your eyes actually
have nothing to do with it. But the feeling is right. Your world
is in your eye sockets, and my world is in my eyes, personal-
ized for each of us. Our eyes contain the world. Did you

know? Out of the five senses, humans rely more on sight than anything else. Ninety percent of our perceptions of the world are based on sight. So it wouldn't be wrong to say your eyes are what connect you to the world. In other words . . . the number of worlds is equal to the number of pairs of eyes."

Worlds.

Yûko had already told Watanuki there were many worlds . . . had shown him as much.

"B-but that means . . ."

"Don't try to hide your cowardly escape by pretending to ask a question, Watanuki. You great big chicken. You understand it already. You know it explains why you can see spirits and nobody else can. Why the world you see doesn't quite match what everyone else does, why that paradox exists. That paradox is simply a difference of vision. Like everyone else, you are seeing a different world. A world in which spirits exist."

Spirits . . .

. . . are in your eyes.

"That's why you always see them."

Watanuki said nothing.

"Likewise, in my eyes I have a world in which spirits and deceit mingle . . . which means that is how I see the world. We both have abnormal eyes, we both have *kenki* eyes, but Basara Bakemachi and Kimihiro Watanuki see different worlds."

What had caused the most hardship and worry for Watanuki was not the spirits, it was the fact that the spirits he saw were invisible to everyone else.

He was not like them.

That gave him a terrifying sense of inferiority.

The same feeling he'd been grappling with today, when he'd looked up at the sky and been amazed.

Nothing he could share.

Nothing he had in common.

But according to the Eye World theory, that was entirely normal. Not just Watanuki, but every single person, shared nothing, had nothing in common with anyone else.

"B-but that . . . that means . . ."

"It's what they call bias, nitwit. People like you and me — who see something other than normal — prove it. Living proof! There is not *one* world, there are *any number* of them, equal to the number of humans — no, to the number of living things with functioning eyes. See? Have you never thought it strange, Watanuki? Of course you have. You were born with those eyes!"

Basara Bakemachi seemed to be delivering some sort of challenge.

"You must have thought the world was crazy."

"Augh."

He had.

He'd lived long enough.

"Then . . . spirits . . .?" Watanuki asked, voice shaking.

Not because he was rattled. Or because he was angry.

His voice shook from fear.

"Spirits are really . . ."

"Only in the world in your eyes. They only exist there! The world isn't crazy, your eyes are! That's why your problem will go away if you learn to use *dōjutsu*. Just like I solved my problems. It is your problem, so this is only natural.

There's no reason you can't do anything I did. It makes me furious just looking at you—it's like I'm looking at myself years ago. Mm? Or do you plan to go on living by leaving everything to other people, causing problems for other people, whining about how things were meant to be, insisting it isn't your fault, and denying the world inside your eyes? Spend your life as a servant. As a slave. Never face your responsibility. Let other people decide everything for you. Blame everyone else all the time, never yourself. You've never done anything wrong. You aren't the one your eyes are causing problems for, you know. It's always other people who save you when you're in trouble, but when other people are in trouble, do you do anything!?"

Bakemachi snarled that people like that were better off dead, but this did not seem to be addressed to Watanuki—nor to anyone else in particular. At the most, it seemed to be addressed at his own eyes.

At his own world.

"Have you ever groveled?"

Watanuki had no response.

"That's an amazing thing. Getting down on your knees to apologize or to beg, you can feel something leaving your body, like your soul . . . I dunno if it's really your soul or just your pride. But I know it's something very, very valuable. Watanuki, do you have anything like that? Anything to lose by getting down on your hands and knees? If you fail, you won't just be unsuccessful, you'll genuinely have lost something? If so . . . then stop leaving everything to others. Stop spending time with Ichihara, stop relying on her, know the weakness of your own heart. Stop doing what you're told.

That thing is a monster that gets into the weakness in your heart—into the weakness in any human heart. Or did you not notice how much of you it's eaten?"

"Eaten?"

That . . . was a fair price.

Something lost for something gained.

Something gained for something lost.

"Don't be fooled by the convenient logic of a fair price, nitwit. Nothing but your own two eyes is ever fair. The more you try to correct what is unfair, the more inequalities you create."

"Inequalities . . ."

Nothing was fair.

Nothing could be exchanged.

No one had the same feelings, the same world.

"You're the only one who can save you."

Wish.

His wish.

Kimihiro Watanuki's wish.

Why? he wondered.

Why did I go to Yûko-san with it, with something so important to my own future?

With my wish?

How can Yûko-san grant it?

"The Eye World theory denies at least half of modern physics, so there's lots about it that's secret and outsiders can't be told. When I write it all down, about half of it'll be lined out in black. My authority only extends to telling you this much. I may already have said more than I should. If I loosened the strings a little more you'd be begging to join me, but if I did that, then it would be pretty hard to say you'd made up your own mind. I'm not like Ichihara. I do not force, I do not threaten. This is all the material I can provide you on which to base your decision. Make up your mind, Watanuki."

"Make up my mind?"

"Will you help prove the Eye World theory?" Bakemachi asked. "Even with nothing shared and nothing in common . . . if we cooperate, we're part of the same group. But I know this isn't something that you can decide easily. Your entire life depends on it. I'm planning on staying in town for a while. Watanuki, come see me again a week from today. In this park, on this bench. Answer me then. Spend seven days in a world with no spirits, and think things through."

Bakemachi stood up, slowly.

The stub of his second cigarette was flung to the ground, ground under his foot like the first one had been.

"So, Watanuki . . . see you next week."

"No, Bakemachi-san," Watanuki said, stopping him as Bakemachi turned to leave. Not getting up. "There's no need to wait a week."

"Mm?"

"I can answer now."

Without waiting for Bakemachi's reaction, he continued.

_____

"I cannot help you."

_____

"Hmm." Bakemachi looked down at him from the corners of his eyes.

Faking a smile.

"May I ask the reason?"

"In my grade . . . there's a boy named Shizuka Dômeki. Grandson of a pickling stone. Something about him . . . keeps spirits away."

"Oh. Sounds like his eyes have an interesting world. So? What about him? Spirits don't go near him?"

"Right. Which means . . . just being near him rubs me the wrong way. Even thinking about him drives me up the wall. For better or for worse, the spirits are trying to keep me away from him—and since you came to town, they stopped. I don't feel irritated by him at all. I even like him a little."

"Hmm. Great. So?"

"But now . . ." Watanuki said. "I'm being annoyed by you."

Bakemachi said nothing.

"If there are no spirits in town now, then this is not their fault—this is how I really feel. I don't know exactly why you annoy me this much, but I can't just dismiss it either. You are *worse* than the spirits."

No "well" or "um" about it.

He flat-out hated Bakemachi.

That was all.

"Huh," Bakemachi said, apparently not particularly shaken by this. In fact, it seemed like he'd expected nothing else. He shrugged. "Works for me."

Watanuki waited.

"Turned me down! Gosh, it's hard forming a group. You can't just get together a bunch of people with similar powers. Go ahead, do what you like. Being hated by people I just met is an everyday thing with me. Relax. I really hate you too."

Bakemachi seemed to think that not being liked by people you hated was good news.

"Sorry I said all that stuff to test you. It'll be too late by the time you work out just what kind of opportunity you clubbed away, but from the look of things, you won't work that out for a long-ass time."

As he spoke, Bakemachi sat back down on the bench, in exactly the same spot. Watanuki looked at him, puzzled, which seemed to irritate Bakemachi.

"The one doing the rejecting leaves first—basic rule of any breakup scene. Kids these days . . . not even the simplest of manners. You make me sad, stupid. You've hurt me—really. Get out of here."

"Okay."

Watanuki picked up his school bag and the plastic sack filled with *nabe* supplies, and stood up. He glanced back at Bakemachi, as if someone had pulled on the back of his hair, but Bakemachi was looking away, sprawled back against the bench, staring at the sky.

Watanuki wondered . . .

. . . before he mastered *dōjutsu* . . . how had Bakemachi's eyes seen the sky? Like Watanuki, had he seen it filled with spirits?

He almost asked . . . but stopped himself.

It was a bad idea. Nothing to be gained by asking. He could hardly find common ground in their worlds or feelings now.

Watanuki nodded to himself for no reason in particular, and turned around. His back to Bakemachi, he headed for the park exit.

When he'd taken about five steps . . .

"Yo!" a voice called out from behind him.

He did not turn around.

"You're gonna live a long time."

". . . . ."

"People with abnormal eyes always have long lives. Long as they don't get killed. I'm afraid you won't die young. I could not be more sorry. Retard. All that life wasted on nothing, at the end of which you die for nothing. Your whole life as a *servant*."

———

Watanuki left the park, never once turning around.

———

There was a woman who did not wish for happiness.

She was afraid.

There was a woman who wished for friendship.

She was not afraid.

Neither one of them was right.

And really . . . neither one of them was wrong.

Neither of them was successful.

They both failed.

But . . . in doing so, they lost something.

Lost something important.

It was not just a lack of success.

What had they seen?

Just as Watanuki could see spirits, both of them must have seen things that only they could see. They must have seen things that they should probably not have seen.

Watanuki would never see what they had seen.

Because those things only existed inside their eyes.

For Watanuki, they were unseeable. Which meant he had to close his eyes to any discrepancies.

He did not think he was right.

He had no confidence, no self-awareness.

Tomorrow he would regret what he had done today.

And those feelings would change the day after.

That's what happens.

But today . . . he would make *nabe.*

"Mm?"

His hand was on the wall before he realized.

He had not walked that far since leaving the park. He did not feel tired at all, but his hand was on the black wall.

Those black walls — walls he knew very well.

Kimihiro Watanuki knew exactly what sort of shop was inside these walls, and exactly who ran it.

Knew only too well.

Well past too well.

"Ha ha . . . what's going on?"

Where had the hundred-yen shop gone?

Had it had nothing to do with Basara Bakemachi's eyes?

Or had Watanuki dreamed the whole thing?

It was a question not worth thinking about.

The shop . . . where things of little value gather.

Watanuki was drawn through the gates, inside the walls. As he had done before, as he always did, he opened the doors, and stepped inside, inside, inside . . .

He opened the last screen . . .

And there was Yûko Ichihara.

Arrogantly lounging on a sofa, a long pipe in one hand, a small cup of sake in the other.

"You're late," she said, breathing wreaths of smoke. "I'm docking your wages."

Kimihiro Watanuki said nothing, just looked into her eyes.

—heartless eyes.

—frightening eyes.

—cruel eyes.

—bewitching eyes.

—hard eyes.

—eyes that looked at you like you were less than human.

—eyes that looked at you from the other side.

—eyes that looked right through you.

—eyes that appraised you.

—eyes that measured the world in reverse.

—eyes that denied the way of the world.

That sort of eyes.

In those eyes . . .

. . . what kind of world was there?

"Mm?"

Yûko crooked her head, noticing Watanuki's gaze.

"What is it? You seem oddly out of sorts, Usotsuki."

"I almost overlooked that, but you got the reading . . . well, not necessarily wrong, I suppose, but Yûko-san— Like I keep saying, excessively mean."

"I swear, I honestly don't wish to say such things to my adorable Watanuki, but I know it's for your own good, so I turn my body into a demon."

"You turn your . . . so you are a demon!?"

---

* *Usotsuki*   Yûko has affixed a different reading to the kanji for Watanuki's name. *Usot-suki* means "liar."

"Feel free to tell me all about whatever happened, Watanuki. If this were *Obake no Q-taro,* I would be U-ko-san."

"A perfect fit!"

"And you would be Shô-chan."

"How normal!"

"Heh heh heh. The key to repeat gags is to vary the formula."

"Then there must be a really big punch line to finish things off, right?"

"Finish? What are you saying. Repeat gags are good 5,640,000,000 times."

"You plan to continue this until all humanity has been destroyed!? I cannot even begin to imagine what kind of joke would make all that worthwhile!" *

"So," Yûko Ichihara said, smiling wickedly.

This was not a fake smile.

It was the kind of smile a human might produce.

"Was there something you wanted me to do?"

"Something I wanted . . . ?"

The question left Watanuki . . .

Not remembering, not thinking.

Not seeing.

"I've never wished there was so much as I did today," he answered.

"Good." Yûko gave a satisfied nod.

"Instead . . . Yûko-san, is there any wish you'd like me to grant for you?"

---

* *Obake no Q-taro*   Comedic manga by Fujio Fujiko about a mischievous ghost. U-ko is a female ghost who has come to the human world. Shôta Ôhara is the main human character, a young boy who becomes friends with Q-taro.

"My, that is a bold move. Trying to play my game? This is the shop where wishes are granted. Ha ha! Am I reading too much into it to take this suggestion as the first step in your campaign to wrest control of the shop from me!?"

"Definitely reading too much into it."

"Yes, this is the shop where wishes are granted. Countless people have come here, bringing countless wishes with them."

"Countless?"

"Yes, nearly countless. At least 200 million."

This was probably a lie.

"Of those, about half the humans gladly, happily paid me a fair price. No uncertainty, no hesitation; they paid their fair price and received their precious wish in return."

". . . . ."

"But the other half were uncertain. They did hesitate, but wistfully, sadly, they too paid. Heartbroken, regretting it, with their heart in their mouths, absolutely sure they would never benefit from it. Like you are now, Watanuki."

"Like . . . me? No, I . . ."

"Both types will have their wish granted. This is the shop where wishes are granted, after all. I do not select my clients. No matter what the feelings behind their payment, as long as that payment is fair, it does not matter. If they have a wish in their heart, I will grant it. But . . . the former type tend to find the wish makes them unhappy, while the latter type tends to find the wish makes them happier."

Yûko did not seem to care either way.

"I don't know what happened to you, but whatever it was, you should have your wish granted while constantly wondering if it's the right thing to do."

Constantly wondering. Constantly regretting. Constantly failing.

Not believing. Not trusting. Not expecting anything.

Just paying the fair price.

"And you said you would grant my wish?" Yûko said. "Then by all means, make some *Hojicha*."

■ ■ ■ ■

And that brings us to the end of this presentation of the Eye World theory as it presently exists.

This is all of it that we can make public at the moment, and I'm afraid the conclusion that follows remains embarrassingly unfinished. In that sense the Eye World theory remains little more than conjecture. ▬▬▬▬▬▬▬▬▬. Therefore, that aspect of it will have to be presented at some later date, but to help prepare for that occasion, I would be interested in hearing what doubts, concerns, or questions you might have. ▬▬▬▬▬▬▬▬▬▬▬. The Eye World theory is not the kind of theory that can be perfected by a small number of people, so I am hoping to hear a number of useful questions based on flexible ideas.

Let me just add one thing: ▬▬▬▬'s eyes represent one common type of abnormal eye, and should not be considered special. If we focus on him too much, our understanding of the theory could become rather lopsided. ▬▬▬▬▬▬▬▬. But the world within his eyes is one I find very interesting. Particularly for people unaware of ▬▬▬▬, they allow an interesting glimpse of a fascinating aspect of reality.

▬▬, ▬▬▬▬▬▬▬, ▬▬▬▬▬▬▬
▬▬▬▬▬. ▬▬▬▬▬▬▬, ▬▬▬▬▬▬▬
▬▬▬▬▬. ▬▬, ▬▬▬▬▬▬▬▬▬
▬▬▬.

I would like you all to remember that a unique world exists in each of your eyes. ███████ and I are not the only ones with strange and unusual eyes. I hope that you will no longer suffer from the delusion that the world in your eyes is the same as that in the eyes of others.

The Landolt Ring was invented by an eye doctor, Dr. Landolt, and is
now used widely in vision tests. The bit is shaped roughly like the letter C. In fact, it is often called the Landolt C, so you might be more familiar with that name. We've all seen it, but few of us realize just how
impressive it is. What makes it so amazing is that it can measure people's vision without any reliance on what they know. After all, if we
used characters like 鬱 or 犟 or 龘 or 鸝 , children would hardly
be able to read them. Many adults might not be able to either. I'm not
even sure we'll manage to print the last two properly. But with the simple design of the Landolt Ring, all you have to know is up and down,
right and left—no, not even that. Children or adults, anyone can get
his or her eyes tested. For the moment, my eyes are still pretty good,
but when I was a child, to diverge from the point for a moment, I once
had a frightening moment in the middle of an eye exam. In a row of
Landolt Rings pointing up, down, left, and right, I was terribly worried that there would suddenly be an O—a ring without any gap in it
at all. Obviously, that would not actually happen, and if it did you
could just say so, but at the time I was not at all sure I could adapt to
such unforeseen and unpredictable events. Perhaps O would be going

---

* *Eye-test characters* Four complex and obscure kanji. *Utsu,* depression; *bisomi,* frown;
atai, rough; *ri, rei,* or *rai,* a Korean oriole.

a bit far, but diagonals might have been possible (I've never seen them myself, but I have heard that some tests use them) and if I saw that, if I perceived that, then should I say so? Or not? I didn't know. If I answered honestly, "Diagonally upper right," and the doctor said, "Um, there is no such ring . . ." then that would be quite a shock. They would think I couldn't see it and had been guessing. Insisting I had actually seen it would get me nowhere. And it would be obvious which of us was wrong. I did once guess my way to 20/20 vision, but I have no idea what I was actually seeing.

This book is a spin-off of CLAMP-sensei's popular manga xxxHOLiC. I wondered what a spin-off novel would be like, and now that I've written one, it's apparently like this. I'm a big fan of CLAMP-sensei's work, and being involved at all was enough for me. It was a fun and satisfying job. So this was xxxHOLiC: *ANOTHERHOLiC: Landolt-Ring Aerosol.* Ah! I forgot to explain the Aerosol part. But I don't have any personal anecdotes about aerosols.

I wish happiness to the sky, the earth, and all of you involved with this book.

NISIOISIN

Born in 1981, the prolific NISIOISIN has already revolutionized the Japanese literary world with his fast-paced pop-culture-fueled novels. He debuted with *The Kubikiri Cycle* in 2002, beginning his seminal *Zaregoto* series, and *Bakemonogatari* was published under Kodansha's popular Kodansha Box imprint. In 2007 came the magnificent conclusion to his twelve-month consecutive serial novel *Katanagatari*—for which NISIOISIN wrote one novel a month for an entire year—also for Kodansha Box. In addition to *xxxHOLiC*, NISIOISIN has tackled another major manga franchise with *Death Note: Another Note: The Los Angeles BB Murder Cases*, based on Tsugumi Ohba and Takeshi Obata's blockbuster series.

CLAMP is a prolific collective of four female artists—Igarashi Satsuki, Mokona, Nekoi Tsubaki, and Ohkawa Nanase—who made their debut in 1989 with RG Veda. Ever since, they have produced a number of hits that shook the manga world, including Tokyo Babylon, X/1999, Magic Knight Rayearth, and Cardcaptor Sakura.